Give Him Back

B.M. Hardin

ISBN-13:
978-1719173124

ISBN-10:
1719173125

This book is a work of fiction. Any similarities of people, places, instances, and locals, are coincidental and solely a work of the authors imagination.

Acknowledgements

I truly thank the Man above for my gift and for the opportunity to live in my purpose and the courage to chase after my dreams. I thank my readers for following my work and allowing me to entertain them time and time again. I appreciate their continuous support and their interaction with me daily in my book club: "It's A Book Thing"

I appreciate you ladies more than you know!

This book is dedicated to all of my readers, family and friends, that continuously listen to my book ideas and share their opinions, good or bad. I am who I am, because of ALL OF YOU! THANK YOU!

Dedication

This book is dedicated Safonya.

Give Him Back

Chapter One

After 5 kids, and 15 years, there was no way in hell that he was leaving me! I'd put in too much time and gained too much weight, just to let him walk out on me.

Nope.

Not today…not tomorrow…not ever!

He'd have to kill me, if he wanted to leave me for her.

And even then, I swore on hot grits and Hennessey, that I would haunt the shit out of both of them!

"But I'm in love with her Lava."

West couldn't even look me in the face. He held the handles on the overnight bag, tightly with his left hand, and the door knob with his right.

"You love her? We both know that love doesn't mean a damn thing to you. I love you. I've always loved you. And look where that has gotten me." I growled at my husband. "What else do you want from me? I know about your mistress, yet, you still have a home. You still have your kids. You still lay in our bed. I still cook your food and iron your clothes. You have it all…literally. But I will not give you to her. Ever."

West finally turned to face me.

He opened his mouth to speak, but I cut him off.

"Everything that you are, everything that you have, it's all because of me. I am your *good thing*, whether you believe it or not. I am the one who has always been there for you. I've always had your back, your front, and everything else in between. And dare I mention your job? You have your job, because of me. Had it not been for me, helping you stage your little fire and rescue scenario, you wouldn't be the well-known, and well-loved fire chief that you are today. You love that job. More than you love me. More than you love anything. And if you want to keep it, then you'll be home in time for dinner."

I turned my attention back to the book that I was pretending to read. I heard the bag that he was holding, drop onto the floor, just as he opened the front door.

"I'll see you at 7."

West closed the door behind him.

Immediately, I threw down the book and hurried to the window. I watched him. West stood on the front porch, for about a minute, before walking down the steps, and shortly afterwards, driving away.

Slowly, I exhaled.

He was gone, so I didn't have to fake it, or pretend anymore. My attitude was all for show. I wasn't okay with his affair. I was heartbroken.

Hearing him confess his love for her, had torn my heart into two. I just hadn't shown it. I wouldn't give him the satisfaction of seeing how much he was hurting me. I wouldn't dare let him see how badly I was broken inside.

But I was.

Inside, I was a mess.

Most days, just getting out of bed was a struggle. I felt unworthy, ashamed and consistently misused. But somehow, someway, I always found the strength to stay. If it could even be called "strength". I'm sure some would classify it as stupidity.

And maybe I was.

Maybe I was just plain ole' stupid for what I'd been allowing him to do. But no matter what I felt, or how he made me feel, the majority of my heart still wanted my husband to love me. For him to be *in love* with me. For him to realize that I was and still am the best thing that has ever happened to him.

Why couldn't he see that?

And why couldn't she see that second place just wasn't good enough?

When would she cut all ties, stop sleeping with my husband, and *give him back* to me?

Once West was out of sight, I picked up his bag from the floor. I carried it to our bedroom and emptied its contents onto our bed. Piece by piece, I placed his clothes back into the closet, his underwear and socks back inside of the drawers and I took his toothbrush back into the bathroom and placed it on the sink.

Before walking out of the bathroom, I stopped to look at myself in the mirror.

It wasn't me.

It couldn't be.

I was about to be thirty-five and though he hardly ever noticed, I still looked damn good!

Brown-skinned, average height, and five kids had done wonders for my figure. I wasn't the scrawny 22-year-old woman that he'd married. Now, I had enough breasts, hips and thighs, to feed a small country. My booty was juicy, my lips were full, and my eyes were my best assets.

And on top of it all, on top of working full-time, having five kids, and stressing over a cheating husband, I managed to keep myself up. Every single day, I made sure to look like something. I made sure to fix my hair, put on clothes, and make up my face, all as an attempt to be someone that my husband wanted to come home to.

So much for that thought.

Most of the time, he barely even noticed.

I couldn't figure out where we'd gone wrong.

It was as though one day, he just woke up unhappy.

And maybe that wasn't it.

I'd always done everything in my power to please him. Maybe he just woke up wanting more. More than what I could offer or give to him.

And then one day, he told me.

He told me about her.

I'll never forget it. It was a Saturday, in February, right after Valentine's Day. We'd had a good time together, all day, and then that night, he told me that he was cheating on me and that he wasn't sure how to stop.

At first, I was angry. And then I was sad. And then I was angry again, and right then and there, I told him to figure it out, get his shit together, and to break things off with her.

I told him to let me know when it was over.

That was two years ago.

And it still wasn't over. And now he was saying that he was in love with her.

In love with another woman. Someone other than me.

West and I met while I was still in college. I'd just turned twenty and he was twenty-four.

Wesley Lewis Mason, was tall, handsome, and had a body wrapped in muscles. And not to mention that he was chocolate. And I do mean, melt in your mouth, smooth and creamy, pour it all over my body---chocolate.

I was instantly attracted to him, as he walked towards me, that day, and offered to pay for and pump my gas.

After listening to a few of his corny jokes, we exchanged phone numbers and that was the beginning of what I thought would be forever.

We talked and became acquainted, and then quickly we moved from friends, to dating, and only a few months later, we found ourselves in love.

The connection that we had was unreal, and on graduation day, at the end of the valedictorian's speech, he'd arranged to come on stage and ask me to be his wife.

I still don't know how he was able to swing that, but his proposal had caught me by surprise. I'd screamed yes, before he'd even finished asking the question.

That was one of the happiest days of my life.

The next was when we were married that next spring. West had given me the wedding of my dreams. He was an only child, and though his father had passed away, he'd left him and his mother separate insurance policies. West had said that he'd never really had a need for it, until it was time to plan our wedding, and boy, did I spend a lot of money. And he never complained. Not even once.

We got married, and enjoyed a few years together, just us. He settled into his career as a fire-fighter, and I took a little time finding my place in the world. Trying to find what it was that I wanted to do.

And then, eight years ago, we got pregnant with our son, Levi. And then for a while, it seemed as though every time that he touched me, I ended up pregnant.

Before we knew it, we had a house full of kids, and though it was an adjustment, I couldn't imagine life without them, or West, for that matter; which was why I hadn't left.

At first, I thought that he was having some kind of mid-life crisis. Or that it was just something about her. I was sure that eventually, it would pass.

And when it didn't, then I thought that his commitment to his wife and kids, at some time or another, would become too much for her, and she would send him home, where he belonged.

That never happened either.

And needless to say, I never expected his affair to last this long. I hadn't expected West to continue to see and sleep with another woman for two, long, miserable years.

At this point, I knew that the future of my marriage was solely up to me. If I'd walked out a long time ago, I was sure that he would've been okay with that. And who knows, maybe by now, I would've been okay too.

Some days, I wasn't sure why I was still holding on, but I refused to say that I was doing it for the kids.

I wasn't.

I was doing it for me.

Exiting the bathroom, I called out of work.

I was a Senior Executive at a well-known Non-Profit organization. I'd been there for a little over five years, and I brought home a six-figure income. We had more than enough money in the bank, and since West paid all of the bills, majority of the money in the bank, was more than likely, mine. I knew that if I ever needed to pack up the kids and leave, I could. And I would have plenty of money to survive.

I just didn't want to do it.

I just didn't want to go.

The kids stayed with my parents, one weekend a month, and then they took them to school that Monday morning, picked them up, and then dropped them off at home that evening.

So, being that I was staying home from work, and I didn't have to do any drop-offs, I wanted to spend some time alone, regain a little focus, drink a few glasses of wine and think.

Unfortunately, I ended up doing everything, except for what for what I'd wanted to do.

After spending a few hours cleaning, washing and folding clothes, and rearranging a few things all over the house, I decided to take a break and get some much-needed fresh air.

I decided to take a drive to see my cousin Thea.

Thea was my mother's, sister's, daughter, and she was my best-friend. She was the type of person that everyone needed in their corner. She was a realist; yet very understanding. She was crazy and spontaneous, but you couldn't help but enjoy being in her presence. She was that one person that you always called and wanted to take with you for a fight. She was loyal. She was unique.

She was my "Big-Tittie The-The"; that's what I called her. Thea was tall and skinny, with boobs that were entirely too big for her body.

"Lord, it's gonna' snow in May," she said, once she opened her front door. I smiled at her as she leaned in to kiss my cheek.

"Busy?"

"Am I ever? I wish I had something to do other than cooking, and cleaning."

Thea was married to a little Chinese man named Ying. He was as smart as a whip. Some big-time computer genius and he worked for a company that paid him more a year, than they could spend in five. And he had Thea spoiled rotten too. She didn't have to do anything, except be his wife. Yet, all she ever did was complain.

"I need to talk."

"Oh God…what did he do?" She immediately knew that it had something to do with West.

"He says that he loves her."

Thea started to make a few noises as she shook her head. "Girl, fuck him!"

The way that she said it caused me to laugh, but infidelity was no laughing matter.

"Why are you even putting up with this mess, Lava? You don't need him."

"But I want him."

"Even though you know, for a fact, that he's out there doing *push-ups* on top of some other chick?"

"As pathetic as it sounds, yes."

She shook her head in disbelief. "I would've fried Ying's ass like a chicken wing, a long time ago, if he was out there sleeping around on me! And if he is, he damn sure better not let me find out, let alone, come home and tell me!"

In a weird way, I'd respected West for being honest with me about his affair. He could've tried to hide it, or chosen to sneak around, but he'd told me. Gave it to me straight. And asked me what I'd wanted to do with it.

I just wanted it to stop.

"You still haven't figured out who she is?"

"Between work and the kids, and his schedule, it's not like I have the time to follow him around all day. I'm always so busy. Hell, he's always busy."

"But he has the time to cheat?"

"You make time for what you want to make time for. He makes the time for her, and then every night, he comes home to me. All I know is that her name is Satin. A few weeks ago, he blurted out her name, because I kept asking him who she was."

"Satin? Well, why didn't you start this conversation with that? It can't be too many women named "Satin", around here."

She picked up her phone. She was searching the web, but I'd already done that.

So many times. I'd also checked social media pages, studying the photos of any *Satin* that popped up, trying to figure out if one of them looked like my husband's type.

I'd always wanted him to slip up, get caught out in public with her, or something, so that I could approach her with a whole, "woman to woman" speech. I often wondered if she even knew about me. If she knew that he was a married man, with kids at home, as young as the age of three. But West was careful. Not once has anyone called me to say that they'd seen him with another woman.

Thea talked to herself, as I searched for my phone inside of my purse. I found it, to see that I had two text messages from West. In one of them, he asked me why I loved him the way that I did, and in the other one, he asked me why it was so hard for me to just let him go.

I'd been asking myself those same two questions, for what seemed like forever, but my answers were always the same.

He was mine.

And no other woman was going to take him from me, completely, unless I decided to give him to her.

I stayed with Thea all day.

We even managed to get out of the house and enjoy ourselves, just the two of us, before it was time for me to go home to my family.

"Mama? Daddy?"

They were already at the house with the kids.

All at once, I heard the sound of ten little feet, patting against the hardwood floors, racing in my direction.

"Mommy! Mommy!" All of them shouted at once.

They all talked to me, at the exact same time, as I kissed each of their foreheads, and then picked up the little one.

My mother entered the room, with exhaustion all over her face.

"Hey, Ma."

I placed Lala down, and they all took off running again, as I took a seat on the couch.

"I put that chicken in the oven for you. The one that you had thawing out in the sink. I have a pot of mashed potatoes ready, and I whipped up some broccoli and cheese."

I smiled at her.

My mother, Dora, was a phenomenal woman.

She'd raised eight kids of her own, and she'd done it with grace, barely even breaking a sweat. My father was there, but they were old school. He worked and brought home the *bacon*; and she took care of home.

She was my inspiration.

"Thank you, Mama."

She didn't hesitate to grab her purse and her coat.

"I love you. I have to go. Your father is waiting for me. Call me tomorrow," she said, waving as she made her out of the front door.

I glanced at the clock.

It was almost 6.

The house was filled with yelling and laughter, as I caught my breath and then headed for the kitchen.

I glanced inside of the oven, to check the chicken, and then I sat in a chair, right next to the stove.

For some reason, I started to think about the first few years of my marriage.

I remembered the day that West surprised me with this house. It was huge, and I told him that it was too big for us. He'd made a joke saying that one day, we would have enough kids to fill it. I guess he got his wish.

He carried me through the front door in his arms. He told me that the house was only the beginning. That life would be everything that I ever hoped it would be. That he was dedicated to keeping me happy and smiling forever. And for years, he'd done just what he'd said.

Every day, especially before the kids, was like a new adventure with him. I never knew what he was going to do, or say, next. Just to put a smile on my face.

And the sex?

We could never seem to get enough of each other. We would do it anywhere, everywhere, mostly, just for the thrill of it. Once, we'd had sex in my parent's bathroom, while she was hosting a family barbeque.

They've been living in the same house for over twenty-five years, so they only have one bathroom, and folks kept knocking and jiggling the doorknob. We ignored them, as we made love on the floor, and then we were cursed out, from here to Mexico, by a line of angry people, once we opened the door.

Even after kids started to come into play, he found ways to remind me of how important I was to him. Whenever he could, he found a way to show me how much he cared.

When did he stop caring?

When did he stop loving me?

Let him tell it, he still loved me; just not enough to be faithful to me. Not enough to stop hurting me.

The aroma coming from the oven, pulled me away from my thoughts, and I opened the oven's door to check the chicken again.

It was done.

After setting the table, I hurried to clean myself up before seven. West would be home, any second now, and I wanted to look pretty.

So, I brushed my hair, put on some ruby red lipstick, and I changed into a dress that was a little more comfortable.

"Kids! It's time to eat!" I screamed on my way back towards the kitchen. I started to fix their plates, and one by one, I placed the appropriate plate, in front of each child's assigned seat.

"Levi, Lonnie, Liam, Layla and Lala! Come on!"

They came running.

I fixed my plate and West's plate and placed them on the table.

"Mama, where's Daddy?" Liam, our 6-year-old son asked.

"He should be walking in, any minute now."

We said grace, and then they started to eat.

I talked to them, and laughed at their jokes, as we ate, but my mind was on West.

I kept glancing at the clock, wondering when he was going to walk through the door.

In between chatting with the kids, I called him.

He didn't pick up.

One by one, they cleaned their plates and begged to be excused from the table. After a while, everyone, but Lala, took their plates to the sink, and disappeared.

I called West again.

He never missed dinner.

He still didn't answer, so, I called the fire station. The one that he was at the most.

"Hey, George. Is West still there?"

"No. He left a while ago. He said that he had to make it home in time for dinner."

I thanked him and then I hung up. I must've called West over fifty times, in ten minutes, but he never picked up his phone.

He was with her. He had to be with her.

Frustrated, I slammed my phone down on the kitchen table and placed my head in my hands.

"What's wrong Mommy?" The three-year-old terror of the bunch, Lala, asked as she chewed her chicken.

"Nothing baby. Mama's fine."

I pulled myself together and once she was done, I started to clean up. A little while later, I got the kids ready for bed, and for the first time, ever, I put them down, and tucked them in, all by myself.

It was 9:30 and still, West wasn't home, and he hadn't returned any of my phone calls. A part of me wished that he was somewhere, dead, but I knew that I wouldn't get that lucky.

I reminded myself, that I was the one who was choosing to stay in this dysfunctional relationship. I'd allowed his cheating, and his disrespect, so I couldn't be angry at anyone, but myself.

I'd always known that it was only a matter of time before he started staying out at night and not coming home. And now that he was so-called in love with her, I knew that with her, was probably where he wanted to be.

I should've given him an ultimatum. I should've left him, in the very beginning. All of the fussing and cussing, and throwing shit at him, had meant nothing, if I was going to stay. If I was going to continue to put up with it. And now this was what we'd come to.

And an hour later, as I got into bed, and turned off the lamp, and still, West wasn't there, I knew in the back of my mind, that this was going to be the first night, of many to come, that he wouldn't come home to me.

And I was right.

It was.

~***~

"It's been three days. And you're still not speaking to me?" West asked, once I got out of the shower.

He hadn't come home that night. Nor was he there by that next morning.

He didn't call or text me for the entire day, but when I got home with the kids that afternoon, he was already there.

The house was clean. The laundry was done. And dinner was finished and on the table. The kids ran to him, asking him where he'd been, and he'd lied to them, saying that he'd been at work.

I hadn't bothered to speak to him.

I'd gone straight into our bedroom, locked the door, and I hadn't come out for the rest of the night.

"What do you want to know? I'll tell you anything you want to know. Do you want to know why I didn't come home? What I was doing?"

I didn't respond to him.

I walked in front of him naked.

In silence, I got dressed for work, and headed out of the room.

"Lava? Lava?"

I walked straight out of the house, after telling the kids that I loved them, and that Daddy would be the one taking them to school.

Mentally, I was feeling mighty low. Emotionally, my heart and my ego were bruised. Still, I refused to let him see what I was going through, but as soon as I was far enough away from the house, I started to cry.

What I was doing, and putting up with, wasn't easy. And at this point, I wasn't even sure if it was worth it.

I arrived at work, knowing that all day, I would have to wear *a painted smile*.

"Good morning Lava."

"Good morning."

I headed straight for my office.

I didn't want anyone to see the red in my eyes, so I shut the door behind me, in hopes of a little peace.

"Knock. Knock."

I guess not.

Tokyo, a co-worker and a dear friend of mine, stuck her head in. "Don't forget that you have three interviews today---for the charity events coordinator position, in conference room E. Your first applicant should be here soon."

"Shoot. I forgot all about that. Can you tell Maxine to print out the résumés for me?"

"Will do." She stared at me. "Hey, you okay?"

"I will be."

"Want to talk about it?"

"Not really."

Tokyo huffed, came all the way into my office and then she closed my office door behind her.

She was the only other person, other than Thea, that knew what I was going through with my husband.

Tokyo was like a breath of fresh air. Sweet, bubbly and religious. She was always positive, about everything, even when the world was collapsing all around her.

She and I could relate because she had a husband that was a piece of work too. He cheated on her all the time, with different women, so, if anyone understood what I was going through, she did. Religiously, she didn't believe in divorce, so she was trying to hang in there, but every day, I could tell that she was about to reach her breaking point.

And so was I.

"Talk to me. What's wrong?"

I shrugged. "What isn't?"

"West?"

"Yes."

She shook her head. "It must've been a full moon or something last night, because Jerell was acting up all night too. We argued like crazy…over something that he did! Well, over someone that *he did*."

She folded her arms over her chest.

Tokyo was a very petite woman. She didn't have much of anything, but she was pretty. Her facial features were strong, but it was something about the way that she wore her hair, that made everything come together.

"Yeah. Well, I'm just sick and tired of being sick and tired. But whatever."

Tokyo and I chatted for a little while longer, and then she headed to get her day started.

Before I could get started with mine, Maxine called in and told me that my first candidate was already there and waiting for me.

"I put them in order of their interview. Janice is first," she said, reaching me the papers, mid-stride.

"Hello, Janice Ingram. I'm Lava Mason."

Entering the conference room, I greeted the middle-aged lady, and we both took a seat. After the first few minutes, I knew that she wasn't the right candidate for the job, but I continued asking her questions, and half listened to her responses.

"Thank you so much for coming. We will be filling the position by the end of next week. Be on the lookout for a call or e-mail correspondence from us."

She shook my hand and I sat down to look at my phone.

West had written and entire paragraph.

After reading the first line that said: "I told you how I felt, but you..." I deleted the entire message.

There was no way in Hell that I was going to let him make his decisions my fault. I don't care what he told me, about how he felt...about another woman!

All I cared about was what he told me that he felt about me!

What he'd vowed to do and be for me!

I looked up, just as she walked in.

"Hello," she smiled.

I had to take a moment to take her all in. She was absolutely stunning! The most beautiful woman that I'd ever seen. And that wasn't an exaggeration.

I was so mesmerized by her beauty, that though I could see her lips moving, I couldn't hear a single word that was coming out of her mouth.

She was Indian, or maybe Latino.

Dark hair and eyes, with envious high cheek bones. She had long, natural, eye-lashes and perfectly arched eyebrows. Her lips were luscious and coated with a bronze matte lipstick and she had a head full of long, thick, black curls. She wore a gold head piece, and a single gold bangle on her left wrist, which pushed me back towards the initial thought of her being of Indian decent. Her dress was black, fitted, yet it had a professional flare to it.

She reminded me of a beautiful painting or something.

"Hello, I'm Satin Gamal."

Satin?

My heart stopped beating, for a second too long.

I looked down at the résumé.

Yep. Her name was Satin.

Please don't tell me that this is her.

This can't be her!

She stuck out her hand for me to shake it.

"Hello Satin...I'm...I'm Lava."

I said my name, wondering if it would mean anything to her. She smiled at me as though it didn't.

I glanced at her ring finger. It was bare.

"Let me take a look at your résumé," I chuckled, uncomfortably. "Okay, oh so you graduated from Clemson University? A southern belle," I inquired.

"Actually, I was born in Cairo. Egypt. We came to the U.S. when I was 9. Settled with family in Long Island, New York. And in high-school, we moved to Georgia. I went off to school in South Carolina, and then I took a job here in Virginia, right after graduation. And I've been here ever since," she explained.

I nodded. "Cairo?"

"Yes. My father is Egyptian. My mother is black. They met while she was on a research assignment. They married, stayed there for some time, and then she brought us all back here."

She flashed her darling smile at me.

I stared at her résumé, hoping not to seem as nervous as I was.

I knew it in my gut that this was her.

This was the woman that was sleeping with my husband.

"So, tell me about your last job. I see that you were an Events Coordinator there. Correct?"

She started to talk, but I wasn't listening to her. I was too busy, mentally, comparing myself to her.

I couldn't find anything wrong with her.

Not one single thing.

She finished talking, and I found something else to ask her, so that I could continue my observations.

Visions of my husband kissing her, and having sex with her, taunted me, eternally, making it hard for me to stay calm or focused.

"We're a very friendly, family-oriented work environment. Husband? Kids?"

"No. Hopefully soon. My father has been trying to arrange my marriage for years, but I wanted to find love on my own. I think I have. We're in love. And he treats me like a queen. If he had things his way, I would be a housewife, barefoot and pregnant, in the near future. He has no idea that I'm even interviewing for this job today, but I love what I do and I'm just too good to waste my talent."

I felt as though I was going to throw up.

"Okay. I think that's all. We have a few more candidates to interview, but we will be making a decision next week. Hopefully, you'll hear from us soon."

She stood up and instinctively, I checked out her booty.

Perky and perfect.

"Thank you so much. Have a great day!" She shook my hand again, and I plastered a fake smile on my face, until she was gone.

Once she was out of sight, immediately, I sat back down and tried to catch my breath.

I looked at her résumé again. For a long while, I just stared at her name and then I realized that I had her address, her phone number, everything, right there in my hands.

I was staring right at the truth.

Though she was more than qualified, there was no way in hell that she was getting the job, but I couldn't help but to think that her, of all people, showing up for an interview, wasn't by chance.

It was by destiny.

And obviously, destiny, had something that it was ready for me to see.

~***~

"Thea, move your head."

Thea and I were parked across the street from Satin's house. The house was big. And I mean BIG!

It was a whole lot of a house; especially for someone who was supposedly single, unemployed, and had previously worked as an Events Coordinator.

There was no way that she'd paid for her house, on that kind of salary.

It was Saturday evening, and I'd asked my parents to babysit the kids. I hadn't spoken to West all day, and when I'd gotten home from running errands and everything else in between, he wasn't there, so I asked Thea if she wanted to do a stake out with me.

"Ain't nothing going on anyway. You sure he ain't at work? Maybe there was a random fire or something somewhere."

"He doesn't work on Saturdays."

After going back over Satin's résumé, I found that she was a little younger than I was. If I went by the year that she'd graduated from college, she'd just turned 30; which meant that she was almost ten years younger than West.

"Maybe she excites him, because she's young and free."

"That's still no excuse for him to cheat."

"She's so pretty Thea."

"And so are you."

"Yeah. But she's like *pretty-pretty*."

Thea shushed me at the sight of her walking towards her car.

"Oooh, she is," Thea commented.

"Told ya," I complained.

Satin was wearing a short red dress and heels. She had her curly hair pulled back into a bun, and even though it was late evening, the diamonds on her hoop earrings, shimmered and glowed like a ray of sunlight.

"Maybe she's going out."

"We're about to see."

She drove passed Thea's car, and then Thea started up her car, and started to follow her.

She drove only a short distance from her house, to a bar...right down the street from the fire station.

"I told you Thea!"

I already knew that she was *West's Satin*, but seeing him, standing by the entrance of the bar, waiting for her confirmed it.

She parked her car and sashayed towards him.

West embraced her, just before opening the door for her, and then they went inside.

I started to pant.

"Don't you dare cry!" Thea yelled at me, as she continued to drive down the road. "I promise you, I'll slap the hell out of you if I see one damn tear! You're the one putting up with this!"

I followed her instructions, and I didn't shed a tear.

For a long while, Thea and I rode in silence.

I couldn't compete with that.

Satin, his mistress, was nothing like me, and apparently, everything that he wanted. Hell, she was everything that most men wanted.

"Well, at least now you know who she is."

"Yeah. Now I know. I wish I didn't. Now I know why my husband can't stay away from another woman. Hell, if I was into women, I'd tap that."

Thea laughed at my joke, but I was serious.

I exhaled, loudly, just as she started to speak.

"Look at it this way. We know who she is, and where she lives. So, the question is…what the hell are we going to do? About her? I have a few ideas." Thea let out an evil laugh.

Surprisingly, her words were like music to my ears.

I looked at Thea and smiled.

"What exactly, do you have in mind?"

****

Chapter Two

"I'll see you later," West said, behind me.

I didn't respond.

After standing there for a while, finally, he walked out of the room.

Needless to say, all of Thea's plans were either insane or illegal, and ended with us going to jail. So, I was going to have to handle this situation all on my own.

I hadn't done anything or said anything, as of yet, since seeing my husband with Satin.

The only time I even spoke to West, was when it was something about the kids. But other than that, he wasn't worth my time or my words.

After seeing her, Satin, I couldn't help but to take a look in the mirror. I'd thought that I was keeping myself together. I'd thought that I was giving him something to look at every day, but with him looking at her, there was no way that he could see past her beauty to see me.

I rushed to get the kids to school, and then I headed to work.

"What do you think about longer hair on me?"

Tokyo, shrugged.

"You don't like weave."

"I know. But I'm thinking about getting some. And some eyelashes too. Mine could stand to be a little longer."

She stared at me. "Okay. What's going on? This is about West, isn't it?"

"No. It's about me." I lied. "Besides, my birthday is in a few days, and I was just thinking that it was time for a change."

Tokyo stared at me. "Spit it out," she demanded.

"What?"

She placed her hands on her hips.

"I saw my husband's mistress the other day. Satin, is her name. And she was a knockout! Very Pretty. Educated. A nice body. And I just..."

Tokyo shook her head. "You don't have to tell me. Trust me, I understand. I went through this phase. In the beginning. Trying to make myself better, to make him notice me, and notice them, the other women, less. It doesn't work. I had to realize that what Jerell was doing to me and to our marriage, wasn't about me. It was about him. And no matter what you do, or what you change, the situation won't. Unless he wants it to. You're beautiful. Just the way that you are."

I beamed at her.

I loved how she stayed so kind and gentle, and full of faith. I envied her ability to be able to go through the worst, but somehow, still be able to see the best.

She and I have worked together for three years, and since I've known her, she's been unhappily married.

She's been dealing with a lying, cheating husband, for a very, very, long time and although she complains, gets upset, and sometimes cries, she always stays.

For better or for worse.

Those were the words that she chose to live by.

Before I found out about West, I used to think that she was dumb. I used to try to talk her into leaving her husband all the time, but she never would. And now, being in the same situation, I guess I understood why.

It's just not that easy.

It's not always that simple.

I knew that she meant well. I knew that she thought that I was beautiful, and maybe I was. But I wasn't beautiful enough.

"I already made my hair appointment. So…" I said to her. "I'm thinking about getting a little birthday lipo too."

"Lava!"

I shrugged and continued telling her about my makeover plans.

"I love it," I said to my beautician, Stacy, later on that day. She'd sown in three bundles of 20-inch long, body wave hair. I'd never been the type to wear weave. I loved being natural, but I was in awe of the change.

"And I like the eyelashes, too. They look so natural, and full."

She smiled at me as I stood up.

"Yes. West is going to lose his mind when he sees you! Don't come back in here, next month, pregnant," she laughed.

I doubt it.

Stacy gave me instructions on how to maintain my hair, until it was time for me to come back in and get it washed. After I paid her, I headed on my way.

I was her last client, and it had taken hours. It was a little after 8 o'clock. West was home with the kids. He'd known that I was going to get my hair done, but I was sure that he was going to be surprised with the transformation.

Seeing Satin's long, curly, beautiful hair, I was pretty sure that long hair was now his "thing". Maybe he would try to "jump my bones" and I was going to get so much joy out of turning him down.

I sat inside of my car, staring at myself in the mirror, impressed with how I looked.

I decided to put on a little make-up.

Make-up was my hidden talent, and by the time that I was finished, I looked as though I belonged on the cover of a magazine.

Stealing my attention, away from myself, my phone started to vibrate.

It was West.

It was getting late and he probably wanted to know where I was. I didn't answer it. Instead, I decided that I was going to stay out a little while longer.

So, I drove around in circles for quite some time.

I even found myself riding by Satin's house. And then at some time or another, I ended up at the bar, near the fire station. The same one where I'd seen West and Satin together for the first time.

I looked down at my clothes.

I still had on work clothes. A blouse, skirt, and heels, but I remembered the bag of clothes that Thea had in my trunk, that she was hiding from her husband.

Her husband, Ying, made a lot of money, but he fussed about the way that she spent it. Even though he didn't mind spending it on her, Thea could do some real damage with three or four hours, inside of a mall, with his credit card. One time, in three hours max, I'd seen her spend almost twenty grand. After that, he gave her a personal card, for spending, but he always fussed at her for buying things that she didn't need.

So, often, she would do a lot of shopping, and then hide it in my trunk, revealing it little by little.

I parked at the back of the bar and went through the bag. I tried to find the least revealing piece in the bag, but even that was a little too sexy for my taste.

Thea dressed as though she was trying to get picked up by a stranger and held hostage. She was always half-naked, and she loved showing off her body and tiny curves. She was skinny, but not the straight up and down kind. Her hips flared out, just a little, and though her breasts were bigger, she had a cup of booty too.

I was surprised that Ying never seemed to have a problem with Thea's dress code, but there had been plenty of times that West had threatened me, saying that if I ever left the house, dressed like Thea, he would kill me.

Humph.

We'll see about that.

I decided on a dress, fishnet stockings, and some of her brand-new pumps, and I changed my clothes inside of my car.

It took me a while to get myself together, but finally, I was out of the car, making my way inside.

I couldn't remember the last time that I'd been inside of the bar or a club. If I had to guess, it was probably around three *kids* ago.

And I had never been to this particular one.

I walked inside, to find that it was a little more upscale than I thought it would be. Nervously, I headed over to the bar, and took a seat on a stool. I'd hoped that some of West's little fire buddies, were there, so that they could call him and tell them that I was there, looking like a *snack*, but as I looked around, I didn't see anyone that I recognized.

So, I ordered my first drink. The music was just my style, and it was crowded for a Tuesday night.

West called me over and over again, and then he started to send me text messages, back to back.

I continued to drink, and I laughed at them.

He acted as though he was concerned, at first. And then he started to curse and question where I was.

The nerve of him.

"Can I get a refill?"

I pushed my glass towards the bartender.

"Long day?"

I scoffed. "Day. Month. Year."

For the first time, I noticed the strikingly handsome man, that was sitting right next to me.

"Come on, now. It can't be that bad," he bellowed.

"Wanna' bet?"

The bartender slid my glass back in my direction, and I closed my eyes, as I took a sip.

"That's number four."

"Excuse me."

"That's your fourth drink."

"Oh. So, you've been keeping count?"

"Yes." Was all that he said.

Over the rim of my glass, I gawked at him.

He was absolutely gorgeous! And that wasn't just the alcohol talking either.

Hungrily, I examined him, from top to bottom, as he tapped on the bar to get the bartender's attention. Politely, comfortably, he made his drink request known, and then he turned his attention back to me.

"So, do you have a name?" He asked in a low, penetrating, tone.

"Lava."

He smirked. "Your real name. Not your stripper name."

"Oh, so I look like a stripper to you?" I joked.

Briefly, he scanned me up and down.

"Well…"

"Hey!" I glanced down at the short black dress, fishnet stockings, and the Gianvito Rossi heels, that I was wearing. The dress was cut so low at the top, that I'd had to wear it with no bra. I guess maybe I did, look a little bit like a slut.

"I'm not a stripper," I snickered. "And Lava is my real name."

He nodded as though he was amused.

"Yeah. I bet it is," he joked.

I smiled at him flirtatiously.

I was amazed of how comfortable I was talking to him. I'd never so much as thought about cheating on West with another man, no matter what he did to me. I'd never even given another man the time of day, or a conversation. But here I was, with a complete stranger, trying to think of something else to say to him.

"Lava." He repeated my name. "I like it."

"And you are?" I asked him.

"Kemp."

"Kemp? Surprising. You look more like a Pablo or Luis to me. What are you? Italian? Hispanic?"

"No. My father is Egyptian. My mother is a beautiful black queen."

I choked.

I'd heard that before. I stared at him.

It couldn't just be a coincidence.

I remembered Satin's comments about her parents, from her interview. She'd said the same thing.

"Let me guess, from Cairo?"

"Actually, yes. But my family has been in the states now, for a very long time. We uh, own this bar. And a few other businesses, here, in Virginia, and in a few other states."

Her brother.

He had to be Satin's brother.

He took a sip of his newly replenished drink, allowing me to dwell on my thoughts and to study him.

His skin was tinted, creamy, like a lightly browned buttermilk biscuit. His hair was as dark as charcoal, shoulder length, and full of lustrous curls. His eye color matched his hair, and big, taunting lips, graced his face, charmingly between his low mustache and neatly trimmed beard.

I appreciated how well-dressed he was in a pair of black slacks, a royal blue blazer, and matching bow tie. A little overdressed for where we were, but I got the feeling that maybe he'd simply stopped in for a drink, after leaving somewhere important.

"Oh. So, you come from a family of money, huh?"

"We do okay. It wasn't always like that. And judging by those shoes, you must not do too bad yourself."

"What? A man that knows his shoes? I'm impressed."

"Nah. Nothing like that. I have a sister. And all she does is spend money on stuff like that."

Bingo.

He had to be talking about Satin. My husband's mistress was his sister. This conversation could get interesting, and I contemplated on where I wanted it to go next.

"So, where's the Mrs? She can't be too far away with you looking like that?" Finally, I managed to say.

"I'm divorced. You?"

"I'm divorced too."

He looked confused.

"Then why do you still wear your wedding ring?"

He looked as though he pitied me, but quickly, the look of sympathy on his face vanished.

"It's new. I guess I haven't really come to terms with it yet." I lied.

He didn't look convinced, but he nodded his head and in unison, we both took a sip of our drinks.

"Well, look at the bright side. With every ending, comes a new beginning," he said.

"Maybe." I said. "Any chance that you could be a part of this new beginning, that you speak of?"

I wanted to place my hand over my mouth, but I didn't want to seem childish. I couldn't believe the words that had just come out of my mouth.

I was flirting. I was actually flirting with another man.

"Maybe." He mimicked my response.

There was an awkward silence between us for a long while. It was as though neither of us could think of anything else to say.

Finally, Kemp stood up, showcasing his height, and lean physique, and he prepared to leave.

The alcohol already had me saying things that I didn't mean, I think, so I just sat there, with my lips pressed tightly together.

"Maybe you should take it easy on the drinks. Maybe call a cab home," Kemp said to me, surprisingly.

Kemp told the bartender that my drinks were on the house, and he ordered him to call me a cab, and see that I got into it, after I'd had another drink or two.

Impatiently, I waited for him to look back at me.

Finally, he did.

"You have a good night, Lava," was all that he said.

And with the conclusion of his words, he made his way through the bar. I watched him, until he disappeared.

I let out a long sigh, and then I devoured the rest of my drink. I ordered one more, and after I finished it, I struggled to stand up from the bar stool.

"Ma'am, let me call you a cab."

I waved him off. "No. I'm fine."

At least that's what I'd said.

I hadn't noticed how tipsy I was, until I started to walk.

I rushed towards the Exit sign, and once I pushed through the bar doors, the cool night air helped me to focus.

Slowly, I walked to my car, knowing that I'd gone way past my limit. I was surprised to find that in that moment, West crossed my mind.

I figured that West must have been coming to the bar, often, with some of his friends, and because her family owns it, since she was obviously Kemp's sister, maybe they kept running into each other, and somehow, sparked a flame. I'm sure that it was hard not to notice her, and West was very easy on the eyes as well.

I wondered if he'd approached her, or if she'd taken a chance and said something to him first.

After getting into my car and locking the door, I sat there, in a daze.

I wondered if there was something that I could've done differently, to cause a different result.

Maybe we should've stopped at baby number two, like we'd planned to. That would've given us more time for each other. More energy. More time to spend together. Like we used to.

Maybe I should've given him more sex. I would try to give it to him, at least twice a week, but most of the time, it just seemed impossible. With the kids, work, homework, cooking dinner every night, taking care of him and household chores, by the end of the night, most of the time I felt like I was about to die.

Like, literally, fall to the floor, heart stops beating, then open my eyes, and be face to face, with my Maker, type of die.

No lie. That's how tired I was on most days. But still, I would try to give him some when I could. I knew that it wasn't enough. West wanted it all the time, every day, if I would give it to him.

Maybe that's why he stepped out on me.

I groaned.

All of a sudden, my eyes became extremely heavy, so I closed them. Immediately, I regretted not allowing the bartender to call me a cab. I'd been up since 6:00 a.m. that morning, and it had to be close to midnight.

"I'm just going to sit here, for a second," I mumbled aloud.

At least that's what I'd said.

The next time that I opened my eyes, it was dawn.

I'd fallen asleep!

I looked around the empty parking lot.

I couldn't believe that no one had tapped on my window to wake me. I was even more surprised that no one had tried break into my car to steal something from me.

I found my cell phone inside of my purse.

Starting the car, I noticed that West had called and texted over 100 times. And he'd must've called around, scaring everyone else, because I had just as many calls from Mama and Thea, too.

Ten minutes later, I was pulling into our driveway.

Instinctively, I glanced at myself in the rearview mirror.

My hair and even my make-up, were both still intact.

Before I could get out of the car, West opened the front door and came out onto the porch.

Surprisingly, Layla and Lala, were already up and came outside with him.

West looked at me. Almost as if he didn't recognize me, as I strutted towards him, still wearing Thea's dress and shoes.

"Where the fuck have you been!" He shouted, finally.

Lala screamed my name over and over again, and Layla said that my shoes were pretty.

"Out. I feel asleep."

"Out? Out where?"

"Out." I growled at him.

"You feel asleep? Where Lava?"

I didn't comment. Instead, I started speaking baby talk to the kids.

"Where!" West yelled and grabbed my arm. I yanked it away from him.

"What does it matter to you? Don't you do what you want to do?"

I pushed passed him.

"Why are you dressed like that? Where did you go? Who where you with?"

I didn't answer him, I just kept walking.

"And you're not wearing a bra! You think I'm stupid, don't you?"

West followed me everywhere that I went, still fussing in my ear.

I headed into our bedroom and started to find my clothes for work.

"Don't you ever do that again," West demanded.

"Or what? You're going to leave me? You're going to cheat on me?" I rolled my eyes and then I answered my questions before he could. "You're not leaving me to raise your kids on my own, and you're already doing the last one. So, unless you're about to tell me that you're going to leave that bitch alone, get the hell out of my face, and leave me alone!"

I walked into our bathroom and slammed the door in his face.

West punched the door and after hearing him mumble a few more curse words, everything grew quiet, and with a smile, I turned on the shower, to get myself to work.

Finally.

I had his attention.

~***~

"Happy Birthday!" Tokyo and Thea walked into my office at the same time.

Tokyo was carrying balloons, and Thea was carrying lilies.

"I picked these up. To keep the tradition going. In case your stupid ass husband was too busy cheating to do it."

Thea was brutally honest. But I was used to it.

"Thank you. And he was gone before I got up this morning, so I don't know. He didn't even wish me happy birthday, and I didn't see any lilies."

Every year, since we've been together, West bought me lilies for my birthday. They were my favorite flowers, and also reminded me of my grandmother, Lilly, who passed away the first year that I started dating West. Every year since then, West got them for me as one of my birthday gifts.

"Well, we're taking you out tonight," Thea said, as though I didn't have a choice.

"I don't know. I kind of just want to be home and relax. Maybe we can go out this weekend."

"This isn't up for discussion. We'll pick you up tonight, around 7. I bought you an outfit. I'll use my spare key to leave it on your bed," Thea said, and her and Tokyo, talked for a little while longer, before leaving me alone.

I was glad to see them go, so that I could focus on feeling sad.

It was my birthday, and West hadn't said one word.

I was sure that he hadn't forgotten. He was just being an ass.

The last two days between us, had been nothing less than horrible. All we'd done was argue. And then we would pretend to be okay around the kids, but as soon as our bedroom door closed, we were arguing again. At this point, I wasn't quite sure what we were arguing about anymore.

My work day passed slowly, and after receiving a call from Mama, saying that Thea arranged for her to pick up the kids for me, I headed home.

West wasn't there, and I was hoping to be gone before he got home.

I found an ivory-colored dress, lying on my bed, with a brand-new pair of Manolos.

Ying was going to get her!

She'd even left earrings, a necklace, and a diamond bangle that looked as though it'd cost more than my car payment.

Impressed with the gifts, I showered and got myself together. I wasn't sure on how to curl my weave, so I pulled it to the side in a bun and added one of my artificial lily flowers, to it.

I looked flawless.

I mean, I wasn't Satin Gamal---but I was Lava Renee Mason. And I was just as beautiful as anybody else.

And I deserved to be loved.

The right way.

Even if that love didn't come from my husband.

"Bring your ass on!"

Thea said as soon as I answered my ringing phone. I headed out the front door. Tokyo was driving, and Thea was hanging out of the backseat window.

"Oooohhh Wee! Hey, baby what's your name? Can I get those digits?" She laughed. I entertained her by walking as though I was strutting down a runway. "Chile, get your sexy ass in the car, so we can go!"

I did as I was told.

Immediately, I noticed that we were all wearing the same color.

"Where are we going?"

"Huh?" Tokyo laughed.

I grinned. "What are you two up to?"

Neither of them answered me. Instead, we talked about random topics, and then we pulled up at my parent's house.

"What are we doing here?"

There were cars everywhere; including West's.

"What can I say? I hate your husband. But this was a nice gesture," was all Thea said as we all got out of the car.

Thea led the way and Tokyo walked beside of me.

"Come on," Thea said, opening the gate to my parent's backyard.

The first thing that I noticed were the lights.

There were lights everywhere. And there were just as many lilies, in every direction. I mean, they were all over the place. In the yard, on the back porch of the house, and even down the middle of the long table that was placed in the middle of the yard. The balloons were the same color as the lilies, and so were the candles.

The crowd cheered once they noticed me.

Everyone was dressed in ivory. Even the kids, as they ran in my direction.

"Who did this?" I smiled as my eyes started to water.

"Your husband," Mama answered my question as she approached me.

I tried not to look bothered, but she could tell. She gave me a concerned look, but quickly hugged me, and allowed me to mingle with everyone else.

Family and friends that I hadn't seen in forever were there. I was happy to see all of my siblings, especially my sisters. It was four boys and four girls.

Drea was my oldest sister. The wise, hardworking, and inspirational one. She was always busy, always finding different roads to success. She was the child that made my parents proud.

Janay was the second to the oldest girl. She was lazy. Most of the time, she couldn't keep a job, but she always had a man. She had three kids, by three different men. In my opinion, she was the most attractive, and she probably had the most-liked personality too. But she was also the one that we called ghetto. You would've never thought that we grew up the way that we did, from the way that she acted.

My sister, Declora, was the one right next to me. We were only ten months a part, and she was a successful single mom of two boys and one little girl. She worked harder, and smarter, than anyone I'd ever met. Whenever she did find a husband, he was going to get scoop her up, and never let her go.

And then there was me. The youngest of the girls, the second to the youngest in all.

"Happy birthday, beautiful!" My sister Drea embraced me, and my other two sisters, joined in, making it a group hug. They complimented me, and asked tons of questions, since we hadn't seen each other in a while, and then they allowed me to move on and greet everyone else.

In twenty minutes tops, I must've hugged at least 100 people. And then lastly, I came face to face with him.

West.

He was wearing ivory, from top to bottom. Even his bow tie was ivory, with small specks of gold. The color against his charcoal skin, was a sight to see, but quickly, I reminded myself, that there was nothing attractive about a man who cheats.

West looked me in my eyes, and I looked away.

He touched the bottom of my chin and brought my eyes back to his.

"Happy birthday, Lava," he said.

I didn't respond.

"I've had this planned. For a while. Before…"

"Before you fell in love with her?"

Before he could answer my question, Thea came and stole me away from him.

"This doesn't change anything. And I'm pretty sure he was about to act like he deserved brownie points or something. You're welcome," she said, letting go of my arm, and heading towards my aunt, her mother.

I noticed Tokyo in the distance on her phone.

I could tell by her hand movements that she was upset, arguing, and as I got closer to her, I could see the sadness and frustration all over her face.

"I hate you Jerell! I hate you!"

She listened for a few second more and then she hung up.

"Hey. Are you okay?"

I could tell that she wanted to cry.

"I'm sorry. I know it's your birthday."

"It's okay."

She looked at me, attempting to smile, but she couldn't. Instead, she started to cry. "I'm going to go, okay?"

She didn't wait for me to respond.

She just hurried towards the gate.

I felt her pain. She was me. I was her. I just wondered when one of us were going to be strong enough to let go.

Tokyo disappeared, just as my sisters came and stole my attention.

It was time to party!

Other than Tokyo leaving, the rest of the night was perfect.

We danced. We laughed. We even did one of my favorite things---karaoke.

They'd ordered or made all of my favorite foods. And created me my own signature drink: *Lava Lush*. Some kind of rum punch, concoction, which I loved.

It was definitely one of the best birthdays that I'd ever had.

My favorite was my 26th birthday.

West had taken me to Vegas.

Doesn't really seem like a romantic type of gesture, but it was. I'd been talking about going for forever, and he'd set it all up. The flight, the hotel, the festivities. I enjoyed it so much, that I didn't want to leave. It was an experience that I wouldn't have wanted to have with anybody else. I'm almost certain that we'd gotten pregnant with our first child, while were there, and did I mentioned that we'd won over $60,000?

Yes! Definitely, one hell of a birthday, in my book.

"We're about to bring out the cake, so that everyone can get going. Folks still have to work tomorrow and it's a school night," Mama found me resting on a bench near the back porch.

"Thank you. I know you helped him plan this."

"You know I did. Your sisters helped too."

She waited for a while, and once I didn't reply, she spoke again. "I don't know what the two of you are going through, but it will get better. Love always finds its way."

"Love? Love isn't what it used to be Mama."

"Or maybe it is. Sometimes, love just needs a little reminder."

"Yea. Like a reminder to be faithful or to come home to his wife at night?" I confessed West's infidelity to her. "Did Daddy ever cheat on you?"

She shrugged. "Either he loved me enough to never cheat. Or he loved me enough to never get caught."

And with that, she walked away.

Shortly after, we had cake, said our goodbyes, and then we loaded the kids into West's Tahoe and headed home.

We drove in complete silence.

Neither of us said a word. I couldn't help but to notice all of the different sounds and chimes that his phone was making, but he never checked it. Never even picked it up.

After the process of carrying in five sleeping kids, finally we headed into our bedroom. I undressed and immediately headed to take a shower.

I closed my eyes as the scorching hot water melted away the make-up on my face.

"Can I join you?"

My eyes popped open.

West was standing there, completely naked, never intending on giving me a chance to say no.

He got into the shower behind me.

I inched as far away from him as I could, but he followed me.

I couldn't remember the last time that we'd taken a shower together. I couldn't even remember the last time that I'd seen him with all of his clothes off.

"I miss you."

I didn't say anything. I attempted to wash my face, but he took the rag out of my hand and turned me around.

"I see you," he said.

Don't ask me why, but for some reason, I started to sob.

For the past two years, I'd been yelling at him, telling him to *see* me. To see the woman that he fell in love with. To see that I was fighting for him. To see that I wasn't giving up on us.

West kissed me. He kissed my lips. He kissed my tears. And once I kissed him back, his hands started to roam all over my body. I tried to fight it, but my body had a mind of its own. *She* wanted him, even though in my mind and in my heart, I could honestly say that I didn't.

"You have to end it. It has to stop," I managed to say, just as West kissed my lips again.

"Okay," was all that he said, before turning into some kind of wild, untamed beast.

West started to bite my neck, pulled my hair, and then he bent me over, and pounded me, recklessly, for what felt like eternity.

I couldn't say that I didn't somewhat enjoy it, but I couldn't help but think about how different it was. Sex between us, was mostly slow, and sensual. Even our quickies, somehow, managed to have just enough passion. But this wasn't passionate at all. This was rough, and I couldn't help but feel like he'd just given *it* to me, the way that he often gave *it* to someone else.

I didn't share my thoughts with him, but they consumed me. Once we were in bed, West fell asleep, instantly, while I laid there, and scowled myself, internally.

"I'll be here for dinner. I should be here by 7," West said to me on his way out of the door.

"Okay." I said.

"Okay."

I watched him from the window, hoping that better days were on the way.

I hadn't slept at all last night, and then this morning, though he thought that I was asleep, he rolled over and kissed the back of my head and then whispered that he loved me.

I was surprised to hear him say it.

"Kids! Let's go."

I dropped the kids off and before I knew it, half of the day had come and gone.

I found myself constantly checking my phone. I guess I expected West to be all over me, but he hadn't called or texted me, at all.

As I do every year, the day after my birthday is when my vacation from work starts. For ten straight workdays, I was off, and with the kids at school and daycare, I thought that I would attempt to do something sweet.

If West was willing to try, so was I.

A few minutes after noon, I stopped at his favorite sandwich shop to get him lunch, and then I headed to the fire station.

West was the chief, but he was often at one particular station, even his office was there, where he handled his administrative duties.

I took the long way to the station, riding past Satin's house. West's car wasn't there, and neither was hers.

Pulling up at the fire station, immediately, I noticed that West's car wasn't there either.

One of the fairly new guys, noticed me, as he was on his way inside.

"You're Mr. Mason's wife, right?"

"Yes. I brought him lunch. Has he already gone to get some?"

He looked confused. "Lunch? He isn't here. He's off today. He's been off all week. Something about it being your birthday and that he was spending all week with you."

I swallowed the lump in my throat.

I smiled at him, as I started to drive away, and then I frowned with disappointment, once I was sure that he couldn't see me.

He's been off of work? All week?

And he hadn't said a word?

Yet, every morning, he'd been pretending to go.

I stopped at a stop sign and I texted him.

I asked him what his plans were for lunch and if he wanted to meet. It seemed like forever, but finally he responded.

"Sorry, the boys ordered in for lunch today. I already ate. I have a lot of work to do. I'll see you when I get home."

At the sight of his lie, I screamed at the top of my lungs, and threw my phone.

****

Chapter Three

"You left him?"

"It was time. Loving him, was killing me. It was just time."

I couldn't believe my ears.

With the way that she thought and the way that she believed, I would've never thought that Tokyo would leave her husband Jerell.

If she could do it, so could I.

I confronted West about lying to me and about taking off from work and not telling me.

He barely had an explanation. Honestly, he hardly even tried to say something that was believable.

He just sat there, while I screamed at him for an hour straight. I asked him if he was with her, and he wouldn't answer me. All he said was that I could think whatever I wanted to think and to believe whatever I wanted to believe.

What?

What the hell was that supposed to mean?

No straight answers.

That's all that he'd said.

He hadn't cared that I was crying and upset. He hadn't cared about my threats. It was as though he was trying to push me into giving up. Push me into letting him go.

I didn't know who I was angry at more. Him for lying to me or at myself for believing him when he'd told me that the affair was going to be over. He was just horny. I'd just been a piece of ass to him, and he'd said whatever he thought that I wanted to hear, just to get him some.

"Where are you staying?"

"You mean where is he staying. I put him out. I'm not leaving my house. And I don't know. And I don't care."

She talked a little more and then I told her that I would call her back once I got out of the car at Thea's.

I was only on my third day of vacation and I wished that I was actually on vacation somewhere, anywhere else.

All alone.

No husband. No kids.

Just me, myself, margaritas and *Hennessey*.

"You look like shit," she said.

"I feel like it too."

"I told you, I'm ready to go to jail, if you are. We can fuck both of them up. Ying will come and get us out."

I shook my head.

"He ain't worth it. And neither is she."

"They may not be worth it, but it'll make you feel good. Hell, it'll definitely make my day!"

"I'm just over it. How would he like it if I was out here, cheating on him?"

"Maybe you should. If you're going to continue to stay and put up with the mess, for whatever reason it is that you keep telling yourself, maybe you should go out here and get you a little something on the side too. I'm just saying. You got mad. That didn't work. Now, maybe you should get even."

I shrugged.

Thea talked for a little while and then she offered to take me out to lunch. I knew that she was going to take me somewhere good, so there was no way that I was going to decline.

Minutes later, we were seated at a nice little outside café.

"Is it me or is that masterpiece of a man over there, staring you down?"

I looked back.

It was Kemp.

The man from the bar that night and the brother of West's mistress.

Once he saw that I noticed him, he smiled at me and headed our way.

"Here he comes girl. Here he comes!" Thea was excited, and all I could do was shake my head.

"I never forget a pretty face," he smiled. I smiled back. "I see you still don't have the courage to take off that ring, huh?" He nodded at my ring finger.

"I was waiting on you, to give me the motivation to."

Uh oh.

There I was flirting again.

For some reason, with him, I just couldn't help myself.

"It would be my pleasure." Kemp flashed his mesmerizing smile. "And by the way, I like this look, so much more than your stripper look."

I laughed aloud.

Thea was looking back and forth between us, as confused as a puppy, trying to catch its own tail.

"Last time, I forgot to get your number."

"Well, don't make the same mistake twice," I said to him. He reached me his phone. I texted myself from his number, so that I would have his and he would have mine.

"It was nice seeing you. I plan on using this. Soon," Kemp said, referring to my phone number. He bit his bottom lip and then he walked away.

Finally, I was able to breathe.

"Oh my God! Oh my God! Who the hell was he? You know him? And you didn't tell me? Does he have a twin? A daddy? A brother? I need answers!"

I filled Thea in on how I'd met Kemp, the night that I'd gone to the bar.

"And you're never going to believe this."

"What?"

"He's Satin's brother."

She scrunched up her face. "Satin? Your husband's mistress? Brother?"

"Um huh."

"Ohhhh, this could get messy!"

"Who are you telling?"

"I like it!"

I laughed at her. "What?"

"How pissed would West be to discover that you are getting your freak on with his mistress's brother? Girl, he would probably croak over and die! It's messy, but girl if there was ever a "get that nigga back" play…this is definitely it!"

She paid for our lunch and just as we left the outside café, in the same shopping center, we spotted Satin going into a nail salon.

"Speaking of the devil."

We walked towards Thea's car and she stopped on the passenger's side.

"Drive," she demanded.

We got into the car and she instructed me to pull in front of the nail salon.

"Stay right here and keep this motherfucker running," she spat.

"Thea, what are you going to do?"

She ignored me and got out of the car.

I watched her through the glass and I got knots in my stomach as she approached Satin and then…

All I saw was Thea's hand go up and slap the hell out of that woman! Then Thea came running, full speed, out of the nail salon.

Laughing and with her big DDD titties bouncing all over the place, she hopped into the car and started to scream.

"Go! Bitch! Drive! Drive! Drive!"

My foot pressed down hard on the gas, and we sped down the street. I started asking her tons of questions.

"Thea! What happened? What happened?"

Thea's laughter was contagious, and I started to laugh too. It wasn't until we were a good bit away from the shopping center that she was able to speak.

"Girl I said: All I want to say to you is stop…sleeping…with my goddamn husband! And then I slapped the shit out of her and ran." She laughed again. "And I wasn't running because I was scared, shit I change my mind…I don't want to go to jail!"

We sped to her house, wondering if Satin was going to try to press some kind of charges or something. She didn't know who Thea was, but I was pretty sure that she was going to tell West that his *wife* attacked her, since Thea had pretended to be me.

We talked inside of her car, until she told me that she had to go and meet her husband Ying.

"I love you," I said to her as I got into my car.

"I love you too girl. You know, I got your back. Always."

With still a few hours to spare, I headed home, just to sit on the porch, all alone and think.

It was late May in Fairfax, Virginia.

The sun was out. The bees were swarming and the leaves and flowers, all looked their best. Soon, the kids would be out of school, and the streets would be filled with little girls and boys; including all mine.

Daycare for the summer, for five kids, was way too expensive, so for the bulk of the summer the kids stayed with my parents. Two of my sisters stayed on the same street as our folks, so they always had plenty of kids to play with, making plenty of memories that they would cherish forever.

As soon as I pulled into the yard, my phone started to ring. Glancing at my phone, I hadn't saved the number yet, but I knew exactly who it was.

"You know, when I left the bar that night, I called myself a fool," he said.

"Oh yeah? And why is that?"

"It was just something about you. You peeked my interest. And believe me, that isn't easy to do."

Kemp's voice was smooth. His words were proper, and very well pronounced.

"I tend to have that effect on people," I joked.

"I can see why. You're beautiful."

His compliment made my heart smile. It was nice to hear those words. Words that I hadn't heard in a while.

"Well, lucky for you, that you ran into me today."

"Yes. Lucky me. I'm usually quite shy. I don't say too much. I don't date much, either. But I knew better than to let you get away again."

I was flattered, to say the least.

"You? Don't date much? Looking the way that you do? I'm sure women throw themselves at you all the time."

"They do. I ignore them."

Over and over again, I told myself that talking to him was wrong, in so many ways, on so many different levels, but still, my mouth kept moving.

"How long have you been divorced?"

"A few months."

"How long were you married?"

"We were married for 17 years. I got married when I was just 15 years old. She was 18. It's common in our culture. Our marriage was arranged. It was more like a business deal between our fathers. She's the daughter of one of the richest men in Cairo. She was coming to the states for school. We saw each other for the first time on our wedding day."

I didn't know what to say, so I didn't say anything. And I guess because I didn't have any questions, he decided to continue to explain.

"My marriage to her, moved my family on to better things. The money was unlimited. I was able to help my family purchase businesses, and homes, that we could leave behind for generations to come. I won't lie. Though it started off as a transaction, we fell in love. We made it work. We planned for babies, and a life-long marriage, just like everyone else. But things don't always happen that way. The older we became, our wants and needs changed. We needed things that we just couldn't find in each other. Neither of us wanted to admit it. Divorce is something that's unheard of in our families. But we did what was best for us. Now, she's back home, in Cairo. I'm here. Looking forward to new beginnings."

"You said that you had a sister. Was her marriage arranged too?"

I was fishing for information about Satin.

"Yes. I have a sister. Satin. And no. She isn't married. She wants to find love on her own. She's always been what most would call the "problem child" yet, somehow, she's our parents favorite. But that's another story, for another day. What about you? Why is it so hard for you to let go?"

I knew that it was my turn to explain. I wanted to lie to him. I'd planned to keep the whole divorce story going, but as soon as I opened my mouth, the truth fell out of it.

"I'm sorry. I lied to you."

Kemp chuckled. "I know."

"Really? How?"

"I wasn't sure until I saw you this time. It was obvious that you are a married woman."

"I'm so sorry. I didn't mean to lie to you. I was just flattered and my marriage…is pretty much over. He's been cheating on me for years. I guess, I just liked the attention. I don't want to waste your time."

"When I asked for your number, I already knew that you were married. If you're cool, then I'm cool. If you're uncomfortable, you can hang up and we never have to speak again. Or, we can be friends."

He gave me a moment to think.

Now that I didn't have to lie about a husband, I figured that talking to him was harmless. There was no telling what he might say, that I could use to make his sister go away.

With my mind made up, I rolled down all of my car windows, and leaned back my seat.

"So…" he started. "Tell me anything. Tell me everything."

Hmmm.

Where should I start?

~***~

I stood by the bathroom door, listening to West talk, low on his phone. He had the water running in the bathroom sink, but I could still hear him.

He was talking to her; in my house, right before he was about to get in my bed!

I was surprised that she still wanted to deal with him, after being slapped by Thea.

West had come home that day as though nothing was wrong. I wanted to see if he would mention it, or if he would act as though there was something about it that he wanted to say, but he didn't. He simply pretended as though it hadn't happened, as though he didn't know, or as though he was waiting for me to bring it up first.

I didn't.

He stopped talking, and then the water stopped running. And then he opened the bathroom door.

And I slapped the taste out of his mouth!

"Don't talk to your bitch in my house!"

He touched the side of his face.

"You don't know who I was talking to," he attempted to defend himself. "And don't put your hands on me, again." West pointed his finger at me. "What the hell is wrong with you, huh?"

Unapologetic, I walked towards the bed, and threw him a pillow.

"Take your ass on the couch."

West stared at me.

"I'm not sleeping on the couch."

I huffed. "Fine. Then I will."

I headed for the bedroom door.

"Lava. How long are we going to do this, huh?"

I faced him. "Ask yourself that question, West. You told me that you weren't going to see her anymore."

"I tried."

"But?"

"But...like I said, I tried."

"Well, I suggest you try harder. You're not leaving. It's as simple as that."

West shook his head. "You can't make me stay, Lava. You can't make me want to be with you."

His comment burned. I almost broke down crying, but I kept it all together and responded to him.

"I don't care what you want, West. I'm sure that the people in Hell want ice water...do you think that they get it? Get over yourself. Leaving me, means losing everything. The choice is yours. I hope and pray, that you make the right one."

Shaking my head, I slammed the bedroom door closed behind me.

Here lately, it seemed as though West always found a way to hurt my feelings. And then I would call Kemp, who made me feel like I could do anything in the world.

Kemp and I were talking all the time.

Every day.

We'd talked the whole time that I was on vacation, and now, that I was back at work, we talked just as much.

The only time that I wouldn't talk to him or respond to his text messages, was when West was home.

I was already crossing the line, but to me, sneaking to talk and text, another man, around my husband, was just going too far. Even if my husband was doing it to me.

If I was being honest, I liked talking to Kemp. There was just something about him. Something different. Something mysterious. I couldn't quite put my finger on it, but I was sure that sooner or later, it would come out or be said.

I sat down on the couch.

The pillow was in one hand, and my phone was in the other. I stared at our wedding pictures on the wall, wondering if I'd chosen the wrong man. Wondering if he was even capable of being that man again.

I recapped the vows that he'd spoken to me, in front of God, and all of our family and friends.

Lava,

You are the love of my life. Making you my wife, is like making my wildest dreams come true. There's nothing that I wouldn't do, nothing that I wouldn't say, to make you fall in love with me, over and over again, every single day. I vow to you, that I'll spend the rest of my life, loving you, helping you, protecting you, and respecting you. Do me this honor and make me the happiest man in the world. Do me this honor, and become my wife, my best-friend, my joy, my favorite girl.

That's what that bastard promised me!

That's what he'd told me that he was going to be, and damn it, he was going to keep his words to me!

I got up from the couch and walked back down the hallway. I opened our bedroom door to see that West was already asleep.

He was spread out all over the bed, snoring, as though he didn't have a care in the world. Watching him sleep, peacefully, made my blood boil.

I wondered how hard it would be to pull off temporary insanity. If I killed him, then I wouldn't have to worry about him trying to leave me.

West hadn't even tried to come talk me into coming to bed, and I couldn't say that I'd expected him to.

Day after day, I was facing my ugly truth.

A truth that I wasn't sure that I saw coming.

My husband didn't love me.

And trying to accept it, just wasn't easy.

In my feelings, and leaving the bedroom door open, I tiptoed back up the hallway, and found my keys and purse.

Realizing that my shoes were in the bedroom, barefoot, I walked out of the front door. Once I was inside of my car, I found my phone, and pressed on his number.

"Are you asleep?"

"No."

"Can I come over?"

I could hear Kemp smiling through the phone. "Yes."

What are you doing Lava?

I couldn't be sure, but as soon as he texted me his address, I put it into the GPS and I drove away.

It was 1 o'clock in the morning. I wasn't sure what I was going over there for. I just wanted to get away. I wanted to be around someone who cared; or at least pretended to.

I knew that having sex with Kemp would make me just as bad as West, and I was better than him, I was better than that, so sex wasn't even on my mind.

I just wanted to talk, and I knew that he would be willing to listen. Over the last two weeks, I'd told him everything; except that his sister was my husband's mistress. I'd told him how hurt and unhappy I was. I'd told him what I wanted, and who I wanted to be. I'd told him some of my desires, and fears, and not once did he judge me.

I drove fast. In a rush to get to him.

I didn't have all of the answers, because in that moment, all I knew was that, with him, was where I wanted to be.

Kemp and I talked so much, that sometimes I would forget that he was Satin's brother. I forgot that I could be using him, to get to her, or to try to get her away from my husband. A few times, I tried to tell him, but then I wondered if there would be nothing left for us to say.

And as strange as it was, I didn't want him to go away.

So, I never told him.

I drove for about twenty minutes to a side of town that I wasn't familiar with. West and I lived well. But the houses that I was driving by, were definitely out of our price range.

They were huge.

Some of them mansions.

And then I pulled up at Kemp's address.

His house reminded me of an oversized doll house. It was big and white, with some strange colored shutters. There was a huge driveway, that wrapped around the front of the house. Beautiful plants and trees.

I wasn't sure of all of the businesses that his family owned, but this house, couldn't have been purchased with money from owning a bar.

Whatever else they were in to, from the looks of it, they were doing well.

Very well.

I was in awe as I got out of my car, wearing only a short spaghetti strapped dress, with nothing underneath it.

"Hey." I said to him as soon as he opened the door.

He wasn't wearing a shirt. Just pajama pants and he had all of his hair up into a high pony-tail, at the top of his head.

Instantly, my temperature started to rise.

I became so hot and horny that I could hardly keep my balance.

Why did he have to look so damn good?

"Don't you look all sexy and tempting," I stuttered, as he closed the door behind me.

"Oh, so you think I'm sexy?" Kemp smiled.

I took a moment to take in my view. I couldn't describe the beauty that was right in front of me. From the art and paintings, to the statues and rugs, all I could do was stare at it in admiration.

"Your house is beautiful."

"Her house. Her parents purchased it with their money after we followed my parents here, to Virginia. They purchased all of these things, whatever she wanted, to make her feel at home. Once we divorced, and she left, and since she never plans to return to the U.S., she signed it over to me, as a parting gift, I guess you could say. I've thought about selling it, all of it, and getting me a bachelor's pad. What you think?"

"A bachelor's pad, huh?"

I turned to face him.

He was so close to me that if I even moved an inch, he would be right on top of me.

"What are you doing here, Lava?"

I breathed heavily.

"I don't know."

"What do you want from me?"

"I...I...don't know."

I was being honest. As honest as I could be.

I wasn't sure. I was lost. I was confused.

"I'm not a good man."

"What do you mean?"

"I have secrets."

"What secrets?"

Kemp stared into my eyes for a moment. We both wanted to kiss each other. I could tell.

"Just secrets."

I smiled at him. "Don't we all?"

Kemp nodded, and then without warning, he picked me up, off of my feet, and wrapped my legs around his waist. After staring at me for a moment, he started to walk with me in his arms.

My nerves went haywire, knowing that this was the night. This was the night that I was going to break my vows and have sex with another man.

Why didn't I feel bad about it?

More than anything in the world, at that very second, I just wanted to feel good.

I smiled at him, and nose to nose, Kemp started to whisper.

"I love your smile," he said.

"You make me smile," I whispered to him.

"I love your laugh."

"You make me laugh," I whispered back.

We stared into each other's eyes, as he entered his bedroom. Slowly, he inched towards the bed and finally, he placed me on top of it.

"It's just something about you," he observed me, as he took the hair bow out of his hair. He allowed his curly hair to fall down, framing the sides of his face.

"I'm scared." I admitted to him.

"Of what?"

"Me."

I was scared of myself and how I was going to feel once we were done.

Kemp didn't reply to my comment.

Instead, he climbed on top of me. He eased my dress up and over my head, exposing my assets and then he started to kiss me. All over me. From top to bottom. He even kissed each one of my toes. The passion, the intimacy, was so intense, that it seemed to suck the air out of the room, and I felt as though I couldn't breathe.

His kisses quickly turned into nibbles and soon licks and sucks came into play. I thought surely that I was going to cum before he even got a chance to put the *head* in.

I breathed hard. And once he started to spread my legs a part, my breathing was uncontrollable, as though I was having an asthma attack.

"Once I start, I won't stop," Kemp licked his lips and since I didn't say anything, he headed *downtown*.

"Ssss," was the sound that escaped from my lips as his tongue repeatedly, *tortured* me.

For what seemed like forever, I whined, I begged, I cried---real tears, but Kemp ignored me. He was on a mission. And he didn't stop until...

I squirmed and cooed and finally, Kemp moved away.

Mission accomplished.

Breathlessly, I tried to speak, but I couldn't.

And he didn't require me to.

He just watched me, as he took off his pants and placed on a rubber. He observed me as though he was the cat and I was the mouse. As though he knew that whatever he was going to do to me next, was going to have me wrapped around his little finger.

I wasn't ready.

And just from the way that he positioned himself in between my thighs, I knew right then and there, I never would be.

He leaned in, close to me. As close as he could go. His breath was hot, and reeked of *va-jay-jay* juices, but I still wanted to taste his lips. And so, I did.

We kissed, passionately, and with a lot more tongue than I usually preferred. I started to become aroused all over again, and just as my clit developed heartbeat of its own, Kemp entered me, slowly.

Still kissing me, every few seconds, he pumped, just once. I started to roll my hips, and still, he made me wait for it. He made me wait for him.

The strokes continued to be long and slow. He would push his inches, deep inside of me and then pull them out nice and slow. Over and over again.

"Oooh." I cooed. As he started to pick up the pace, but just a little. The pleasure that he was giving me, couldn't be put into words.

Kemp kept his eyes locked on mine, as we both breathed in between moans. He grinded inside of me, making every swirl, every pump, more intoxicating than the last.

"Oooh. Yes. Yes!"

I couldn't stay quiet, even when I tried.

My body felt as though it was on fire. We were sweating so much that our bodies were starting to stick together.

My fingernails sank deep into his lower back, as the creams of my satisfaction started to bubble inside of me, begging me to set them free. And I could tell that he wasn't too far behind me. His body stiffened, and I knew that he couldn't take it anymore, either.

It was time to release.

He stroked one last time, and together, we both moaned.

"Ahhhh," we hummed in unison.

Heavily, we both struggled to catch our breaths.

I wanted for him to get off me, but for a while, he just stayed there. Looking at me. Smiling at me.

"What?" I asked him with a grin.

"Nothing." Kemp kissed me, before getting off of me.

I laid on my back with my legs and arms, stretched out wide, while he headed towards the bathroom.

I had never experienced anything like that, with anyone, especially not with my husband, and in that moment, all I could think about was when he was going to do it to me again.

I heard the toilet flush, and soon Kemp strutted back towards the bed. He found his place behind me and pulled me close to him.

"I tore that ass up!" He bragged, and I burst into laughter.

"Really?"

"What? It's true." He laughed and then kissed the back of my neck, just as I closed my eyes.

It felt good.

Being here, with him. It felt right, even though it was dead wrong. I was someone else's wife.

Still not feeling as guilty as I should've, at some time or another, I must have fallen asleep, because I woke up to the room being pitch black.

I found my phone on the nightstand.

It was 4:47 a.m.

I touched beside of me.

Kemp wasn't there.

Groaning, I rubbed my eyes and wobbled out of the bedroom.

"Kemp?"

The entire house was dark.

He wasn't in the kitchen, or the living room, or any of the other bedrooms.

I headed for the window.

His car was gone.

I found my purse, and my keys, and I headed out of the house to go home.

Where in the hell did he go?

~***~

After the first time, it was a walk in the park.

I found myself having sex with Kemp, every other day, and I just couldn't seem to stop. I was going to see him on my lunch breaks. I was meeting him, at the bar, to have sex in his office. I'd always wondered if Satin would pop up or if West would drive by the bar and see my car, on the way to the fire station, but I was so infatuated with Kemp, that for the most part, I didn't care.

"I have a secret," I said to Thea and Tokyo.

West had taken the kids to see my parents and I called an emergency meeting. I needed to have an intervention. I needed them to remind me that I was better than West and I needed them to tell me that what I was doing was wrong and that it needed to stop.

"What?" Thea asked impatiently.

I exhaled. "I've been having sex with Kemp."

Thea squealed.

"What? Who is Kemp? The sexy brother? Of West's mistress?" Tokyo asked. I nodded. I'd filled her in, a while ago, that he and I were being friendly.

"I know. I know. It's wrong. It doesn't make me any better than him."

"Not to mention that y'all are keeping it in the family," Thea laughed.

"It's not funny Thea!"

She laughed so loud and outrageous that Tokyo started to laugh too.

"Shit. Don't ask me to stop you. West deserves it. Screw him! Well, I mean, keep screwing Kemp! I'm glad that you're giving him a dose of his own medicine. Even though he doesn't know it. All I want to know is…is it good?"

I was embarrassed.

"Well is it?" Tokyo asked. She was looking so much better, happier, these days, since she'd left her husband. That could be me, but I was playing.

"Girl…it's…it's…so...damn…good!"

"Damn! That good huh?" Thea screamed. "Oh, and I bet his sexy ass real nasty too? Come on, I want details. All of them. And don't leave nothing out."

I told them what I wanted them to know, and then I turned the conversation into a more serious tone.

"I would've never thought about cheating on West. I don't like it. I don't like how his affair has changed me."

"Then do something about it." Tokyo said. "Leaving Jerell was the hardest thing that I've ever had to do. Something that I never thought that I would do. But it was the best thing that I could've ever done. Maybe it's time to leave. Maybe it's time to let go."

"Or it's time to start fucking some shit up! Shit, don't let no other woman run you away from your own husband! Make her give his ass back! Show up. Show out. Stop watching from a distance, tolerating this mess. You know who she is. You know where she lives. Make that bitch uncomfortable! Everywhere that she goes, if I were you, I would show up. She'd get so tired of seeing my ass that she'll start begging his ass to go home! My opinion---don't walk away unless you are 100% sure that that's the best thing for you to do. And if it ain't...then it's time to start a war!"

Thea took a bite out of her chicken. Tokyo shrugged as if to say that maybe Thea was right.

I wasn't sure what to feel.

I wasn't sure of what to do.

But I knew that before I could do anything, I had to get rid of the distraction.

I had to get rid of Kemp.

Even though I didn't want to.

Sex with him was nothing less than amazing, but here lately, once we were done, I felt horrible. At first, it was good, and I was angry, and I felt like I was getting back at West, but after all of those feelings were gone, I just felt bad.

After leaving the girls, I asked Kemp if he could meet me. He told me that he was at the bar, so I headed in his direction.

"You look beautiful," he said at the sight of me. "Come in and close the door."

The bar was empty, other than a few workers, since it was mid-day, and he was in the office. He appeared to be doing some kind of books.

"I just wanted to talk to you."

"And you couldn't do it over the phone, so that only means one thing. You're coming to tell me that what we have, has to end."

"Yes."

"And that you feel guilty, and that you never expected things to go so far."

"Yes."

Kemp got up out of his chair and walked towards me. Immediately, my body tensed.

"You love him. And I was just an outlet. This isn't you. Cheating isn't who you are."

I breathed heavily as he towered over me.

"Yes."

He stood there, as close as he could get to me. Finally, he stepped back.

"Okay."

That's it?

No "one more time for the road" sex?

No "I wish we could be more" conversation?

"My number won't change. If you need me. For anything. Call me," Kemp said. He touched the side of my face and then he turned around.

"That's it?"

"Yes. That's it. I can't and won't force anything. I told you that from the beginning. Believe it or not, getting attached to you is a lot for me too. I'm okay with whatever you choose. You know my number. Use it whenever you want or need to."

He was a little too nonchalant for my liking.

Although we talked all the time, he always seemed to be hiding something. I was pretty sure that it was something illegal that he was tied up in, but I'd never asked him.

Not knowing what else to say, or if there was anything else to say at all, I walked out of the office and out of the bar.

"Hey, Lava, right?"

It was her.

Satin.

I froze.

I had a million things that I wanted to say. Threats I wanted to make. I even thought about grabbing her by the neck and telling her to get some business about herself and go find her own damn man!

But I just stood there. Unable to speak.

"Remember? From the job interview? You guys didn't call me back, so I'm assuming you went with someone else. That's okay though. What are you doing here?" She smiled at me, genuinely.

She had no idea who I was.

She had no idea that I was West's wife.

But even if she hadn't known before, thanks to Thea, now, she knew that he was married, if she was still seeing him, which I was pretty sure that she was.

Just as I opened my mouth to tell her to stay the hell away from my him, her phone ranged, and she smiled at it and placed it on her ear.

"Hey baby. I missed you."

She turned away from me and walked into the bar. I stood there. Boiling with rage, as I took my phone out of my pocket. I called West and listened to it ring.

And ring.

And ring.

And ring.

And of course, he never answered.

~***~

West hadn't been home since Friday.

And I hadn't called him. Not even once, until now.

"West. You need to call me back. Lala has a fever of 105. The other kids are with Mama and Daddy and we are on our way to the emergency room," I said to his voicemail.

I glanced at our daughter in my rearview mirror in pain.

"Okay, baby. We're almost there."

I tried calling West again, as I got out of the car, and before picking her up.

Still, no answer.

"It's a good thing that you brought her in when you did. We've detected a small blockage, a cyst, on her ovary. We're going to have to take it out, immediately. We need to do surgery."

I placed my hands over my mouth and spoke through my fingers.

"But she's going to be okay? Right?"

"I'll do everything to make sure of that. We're going to go in and try to remove the cyst, without having to take out her ovary. Worst case scenario, we'll have to take the ovary, but we are hoping that we've caught it soon enough."

I started to cry.

My poor baby.

The doctor allowed me to go in and kiss her, and then they wheeled her away. I sat down in a chair, and I called West again.

He still wasn't answering.

I'd left voicemails, and sent text messages, but he wasn't responding.

I called the fire station.

"By chance he isn't there is he?" I asked his friend George.

"You know he's off on the Saturday's and Sunday's. But he hasn't been in since Thursday," George said.

I hung up without saying goodbye.

I called West again.

I listened to the phone ring, and it was as though something snapped inside of me, once I heard the beep sound to leave a voicemail.

"I hate you. And I wish that you, both of you, were dead!" I growled and then I hung up.

The scary part was that I'd meant, just what I'd said.

Allowing my thoughts to consume me, I just sat there. Angry.

Scared for my little girl.

With tears streaming down my face.

When my phone started to vibrate in my hand, I assumed that it was West's sorry ass, but it wasn't.

It was Kemp.

"You were on my mind," he said, once I picked up the phone. "You don't have to say anything. You can just sit here, for a while, and then hang up."

Ignoring his instructions, loudly, I started to sob. It took a while, but I managed to tell him what was wrong. He knew everything about what was going on in my marriage, other than knowing that the mistress was his sister, so, I didn't hold back with my thoughts about West.

"I hate him, and I wish that he was dead."

"Be careful of what you wish for." Kemp warned.

"I'm serious. I'm tired of him! I hate him!"

Kemp gave me a few moments to continue sobbing before he spoke again. "I'm here. I'm right here. I'll come down there or I'll stay on the phone with you, all night, if you want me to."

"Okay," I sniffled.

Kemp started to talk, about random things, just to keep me company. A few hours went by, and we talked and talked, until finally, the doctor came out to tell me that Lala was fine and that she'd made it through the surgery.

They'd had to remove her entire left ovary, but she was expected to make a full recovery.

Kemp heard the good news and told me to tend to my child, and to call him when I could, or if I needed anything else. I thanked him from the bottom of my heart, as I scooted a chair beside Lala's bed.

Hanging up the phone, I grabbed her hand and she opened her eyes.

"Mommy," she said.

"Yes baby. I'm here."

"Where's Daddy?"

I smiled at her, but instead of responding aloud, I answered her question in my head.

Daddy is dead baby. Daddy is dead!

****

Chapter Four

"Stop it Lava!"

I twirled the bat in my right hand.

"So, some tramp was more important than your child, right? You were so caught up, that you couldn't come and see about your daughter, huh?"

I stopped twirling the bat and prepared to swing.

"No. Lava, come on now. I didn't see my phone."

"Why?"

West didn't answer.

"I said why! What, because you were screwing her? I'm sure that's what you were doing! Be a man and say it!"

He stared at me, but still, he said nothing.

I nodded my head.

"Fine. Don't answer me then!" I swung the bat with all of my might, shattering the driver's side window of his jeep.

"Lava!"

West walked towards me, but I swung the bat in his direction, just barely missing him.

"Don't come near me! I'll knock your damn head clean off your shoulders! Don't come near me!"

West halted.

"She could have died. Our baby could've died! Anything could've gone wrong and you wouldn't have been there! All because you were laid up, somewhere, with someone, doing something, that I'm sure you weren't supposed to be doing in the first place!"

Crash!

The glass from me breaking the back window, hit the pavement of the driveway.

West screamed.

"I didn't know that was going to happen! I would've been there! I would've been there! I love my kids, and you know that, so why are you tripping? I'm sorry, damn! I'm sorry!"

"Oh, you're not sorry yet! But you will be!"

My mother was standing on the front porch, ordering the kids to stay inside. Folks were coming out of their homes, cars were stopping in the middle of the street, but I didn't care.

I was sick and tired of being sick and tired!

"You love your kids, you say, but you've been gone from home for days! You didn't even call to check on them, not even once! You care about her more than me! More than all of us!"

"No, Lava! No! That's not true."

"Don't you lie to me!" I walked around to the front of the Tahoe and threatened to smash the front window.

"Lava." Finally, my mother spoke to me. "That's enough," she said calmly.

I shook my head.

Sweat was racing down the sides of my face. All of a sudden, I started to feel dizzy.

"It's not enough, until I say it's enough!" I prepared to swing the bat, but my arms were stuck. I couldn't get them to move. Instead, I started to fall backwards.

The bat hit the ground, and everything moved in slow motion as my body hit the ground too.

I could hear both West and Mama screaming my name, but they sounded so far away. And then everything got quiet. Everything went black. Everything was still.

"You're about six weeks. Judging from the size and measurements, I'll say that conception date was around the 18th of last month.

Both West and I seemed to be calculating.

"That night in the shower. My birthday," I frowned, wishing that I'd never let him touch me.

Though I'd been fooling around, I was sure that it was my husband's baby because I wouldn't have dared to sleep with Kemp, without protection.

I never even had to mention it. He was always prepared.

"What a great birthday gift," Dr. Moses implied.

"No. Not really," I mumbled. West looked at me and I rolled my eyes.

"What if we wanted to terminate the pregnancy?"

"We're not killing the baby, Lava," West spoke up.

I ignored him and stared at Dr. Moses, awaiting his response.

"Well," he cleared his throat. "There are several options."

"Explain them to me, please."

West talked the entire time that the doctor was talking, but I didn't care what he thought or what he had to say.

It was my body. And I didn't want another baby.

Especially not by him.

"With you fainting, if you choose to keep the child, you need to get plenty of rest over the next few days."

"Thank you. I'll definitely call to schedule one of the termination options soon."

The doctor said a few more words, and then he told us that we could go.

We walked towards my car and I walked around to the driver's side.

"You don't need to drive right now. Let me drive you."

Ignoring West, I got inside of my car. He stood there for a while after I slammed my door shut and then he started to head towards the passenger side.

I locked the doors.

"Open the door Lava," he said pulling at the handle.

I started the car and with him still yanking on the door handle, I started to pull off.

I didn't even bother to glance back at him standing in the middle of the parking lot.

He could find his own way home.

Just my luck!

Finally, I was fed up, and now I was pregnant!

My phone was ringing off the hook.

I didn't want to talk, to anybody…except for Kemp.

I hadn't spoken to him in three days; since the day that Lala had her emergency surgery. He hadn't attempted to reach out to me, and I was sure that it was because he thought that I was busy with my child.

Or maybe it was because he was busy. Or maybe he just didn't want to. Either way, I found myself driving towards his house.

With him on my mind, suddenly, I made a U-turn.

There was someone else that I'd rather go see.

The one. The only.

Satin.

It was time for her to feel my wrath, just as West had. The games, the trying to wait things out, hoping that they worked themselves out, were over!

If I was going to carry another one of his big-headed ass babies, I'd be damned if he was going to continue having an affair!

No. Over my dead body…or hers!

Once I arrived, I stormed up her front porch steps.

Banging my fists against the door. After a minute or so, finally, the front door opened.

But it wasn't her.

"I'm looking for Satin!" I yelled at them.

The husband and wife looked frightened.

"Our landlord?"

I looked at them as though they were speaking some kind of foreign language.

"We just moved in a few days ago. This is one of five houses that she owns. She'd told us that she'd been living here, until her new house was finished being built, which was why we had to wait to move in. We moved in last weekend."

I rolled my eyes and didn't bother to say anything else. I was disappointed.

Not only because I wouldn't be able to tell her what was on my mind, but also because now, if West decided to sneak off, I wouldn't know where to find him.

I wondered if that's why he'd been away all weekend. Helping her move out of this house and move into her new one.

Mama's face appeared on my phone as soon as I was back in the driver's seat. She was probably ready for me to get my kids, especially Lala, who was in bed, trying to heal.

I wondered how much they'd seen, or if they'd seen or heard anything at all. I'd worked overtime to shield them from the hurt and pain that I was going through, and I was disappointed in myself that I hadn't been able to maintain the charade for their sake.

I picked up my phone to return my mother's call, but just as I was about to, a text message from Thea popped up.

Ying is out of town tonight. I got wine!

I didn't call my Mama or bother to respond to Thea.

I was on my way.

"Oh, hell no! You're pregnant? Give me that glass!"

I moved my glass of wine out of Thea's reach.

"No! I need this. And I'm not keeping the baby anyway."

"Why not? Is it West's?"

"Yes."

"Are you sure?"

"As positive as those two lines were on that stick."

"Then fuck him and her! That's your child. Hell, look at it this way, you could be me. I been riding the wheels off of my husband's dick for years and I can't seem to get pregnant, no matter how hard we try. Be grateful. All of us can't be fruitful, and multiply, and all that other shit."

Thea took a sip of her wine.

"I don't know Thea. The way that I feel…"

I paused.

"Say it," she said, taking another sip.

"I just want him and her to feel all of the pain that I've been going through these past two years. To feel the pain that I felt that day at the hospital. I swear, when he wasn't picking up his phone, I was praying that it was because he was dead. I literally prayed for it. Why can't he just die? And then I won't have to worry about Satin, or any other woman taking him away from me."

I knew that I could be open and completely honest with her. I knew that she would understand.

Thea had a secret.

Thea killed her mother's husband.

For years, he touched her, molested her, and her mother, my aunt, didn't do a thing. She told everyone that Thea was lying. She'd said that Thea just had an overactive imagination. But I knew that Thea was telling the truth.

I remembered the night that she told me that she was going to do something about it. It was years after she was out of their house. Years after it had all happened, but Thea struggled with forgiving him. She struggled with letting men get close to her, because of him. She'd had trust and intimacy issues, all because of what he'd done to her.

And then that night, Thea told me that she thought that she would feel better if he was dead.

So, she killed him.

She'd followed him, and while he was having sex with a teenage prostitute, in his car, behind an abandoned building, Thea shot him.

She was so scared, yet so relieved, that night that she'd called me to come out of my house, and to sit in her car with her. She was dressed in all black, wearing a hat and a hoodie, with a black bandana covering half of her face. She'd said that the gun wouldn't trace back to her, and that she had someone that was going to get rid of it for her.

I didn't know what to feel about what she'd done, and I was probably more afraid of what was going to happen to her then she was.

She felt as though everything was going to be okay, stating that all she had to worry about was the witness.

The girl.

She wasn't sure what she was going to say, but luckily, the girl had said all of the wrong things.

The girl was so high, that she told the police that it was a man, wearing a black hoodie that shot him, but it wasn't a man at all.

It was Thea.

And because of the witness's statement, one ever came looking for her. No one ever suspected her involvement. She'd gotten away with murder, and I hated to say it, but life, for her, after that, had been better ever since.

"I think you're just angry. You don't want West to die," she poured another glass of wine.

I thought about her words.

I took a sip of wine before responding.

"I don't know. I feel like I do. But maybe I don't. I mean, he is the father of my kids. But what about her? What if I killed her? Would you help me?"

Thea froze for a moment.

Instead of drinking the glass of wine that she'd just poured, she picked up the bottle and started to chug it.

"Trust me, you don't mean that."

I looked Thea dead in her eyes.

"But what if I do?"

~***~

"You shouldn't be here," Kemp said.

"I know."

We stared at each other for a while. He moved to the side to let me inside, but I just stood there.

I was pregnant.

And I was going to the doctor, in just a few, to tell him that I was going to keep it.

If I had sex with Kemp, while carrying West's baby, I would never be able to wash away the *slut* or the shame.

It had been weeks, since I'd seen him, and I just wanted to stand there.

And look at him.

Before I said goodbye.

"Do you want to talk about it?"

I shook my head. "No."

He stared at me.

"I want you. Do you want me?"

"No."

I lied.

"Every time that I see you…"

Kemp started to walk backwards.

I could see that he was starting to get aroused, through his pants, and then slowly he started to unzip them.

He continued walking backwards, keeping his eyes on me, until the back of his legs hit up against the couch. He sat down and freed himself.

"Come here," he said.

I shook my head no.

"I want you to come in and take a seat over there."

He nodded towards the single chair, right across from him.

Still shaking my head no, my feet started to move as I walked into his house, leaving the front door wide open. I took a seat in the chair.

"Take your panties off," Kemp roared.

I looked at him like he was crazy.

"Take them off," he said again.

"Kemp, we can't have sex. I'm…"

"We're not having sex…with each other. Take them off."

I tried to say no, for as long as I could, but watching him, stroke his *joystick*, made it hard for me not to get in the mood.

Before I realized it, I was stepping out of my panties, and standing in front of the chair, waiting for his instructions.

"Sit down. And open your legs."

I opened my legs.

He hissed and started to nibble on his bottom lip, at the sight of *her*.

"Touch *her*."

"What?"

He continued to stroke himself.

"I want you to look me in my eyes and touch *her*."

I was turned on, to say the least.

West hated when I pleased myself, even when we were on good terms. If I bought a new toy, and if he found it, he would simply throw it away, without telling me; until I went looking for it and would ask him where it was.

As instructed, I started to touch myself.

"Look at me," he demanded.

I locked eyes with him.

My fingers found my spot, and I started to move them around.

Kemp kept his eyes on mine, as he moaned.

I started to moan, and as hard as it was to stay focused, I refused to take my eyes off of him.

We kept our eyes on each other, as we filled the room with noises. The breeze from outside, chilled the room, and caused Kemp's curls to blow teasingly all over his head.

And I almost lost it!

My body started to shiver, and I heard Kemp say…

"Come on."

And just as he'd commanded me…

I *came*.

Breathing heavy, we both continued to look at each other as I stepped back into my panties and as he got himself together.

Suddenly, Kemp's phone started to ring.

He answered it.

He listened for a while.

"Yes. Satin was supposed to be there today."

My eyes grew wide at the mention of her name.

"Okay. I'll be there in ten."

He hung up the phone, reached to the right of him, grabbed his keys and then I followed him to, and out of the door.

"I'm sorry. I have to go. My sister was supposed to take a meeting, but she didn't show up."

Kemp complained about Satin as he walked towards his car. I followed him.

"I tell you, that girl doesn't ever do what she's told. She's hard-headed."

And a whore, I thought.

"She can't be that bad."

"She can be. She's that one family member that you think life would be so much better without them...until it almost is. I remember, once, she had a bad allergic reaction to peanuts, and we almost lost her. She'd been a pain in my ass, since we were kids. I always covering up her mistakes and taking the blame when she didn't do something that she was supposed to do. But watching her, on that bed, I couldn't imagine life without her. Until she got over it and went back to her usual self again. I don't mean to ramble. You have tons of siblings. I'm sure that you understand."

"Believe me, I do."

Janay was that sibling for me.

She and I were always going at it. You would've thought that we hated each other. I didn't hate her. I just didn't like her. We had absolutely nothing in common. And when we were younger, all we ever did was fight.

Nowadays, as we got older, we simply just stayed out of each other's way.

But still, I loved her.

Kemp smiled at me.

"I won't ever see you again, will I?" He asked. I touched the side of his face.

"No."

It was fun while it lasted.

I wished that we'd met in another life, where I wasn't married, where I didn't have five kids…and one on the way. Where he wasn't the brother of my husband's mistress.

I walked away from him, glad to have met him, glad to have experienced with him, but it was time to get back to what mattered the most.

My family.

I was about to put my all into forcing my husband to get his act together. And that meant that I had to clean up my act too.

I drove in silence.

It had been a little while, since the big showdown, between West and I, and since finding out that I was pregnant.

And though I was sure that he was probably still communicating with Satin, for the most part, he had been staying at home.

He'd gotten his car fixed, and then one day he'd pissed me off, and I'd smashed the driver's side window out again. I was constantly fussing at him and cursing him out, and I knew that it wasn't doing anything, but making things worse.

West wasn't even sleeping in the bed with me. He was sleeping in our son's bedroom.

Honestly, I didn't want to fuss and fight with him, I really didn't, but it was hard not to. Especially, when it was so obvious that he didn't want to be there. A blind man could see that he wasn't where he wanted to be.

But I didn't care.

It was where he was going to be.

Forever.

I glanced down at my vibrating phone.

It was my sister Drea.

"Hey, I was just calling to check on you. Ma told us all what happened, well, she told us just a little. I called you, a few times, for about two weeks, but you never answered. I was going to come by, but I never seemed to get around to making it over there."

"Sorry, I've just been going through a lot."

She told me that she understood, but she kept her conversation short and sweet. She told me if I ever needed anything to call her, and then she was gone.

Drea, as well as my sister Declora, was always busy.

I had a job too, but they had careers.

Drea was a district attorney, and Declora was VP of Marketing and Sales for a product development company.

I got along well with both of them, though I never saw them. It was always a hassle, just to get them on the phone.

Surprisingly, I was okay with that though, because even though I had sisters, I'd always been closer to Thea.

I threw my phone into the passenger seat.

West was home with the kids, and I'd told him that I had a doctor's appointment, an hour early, just because I knew that I would be stopping by to get one last look at Kemp.

Now, I was running late, and had to show with a dirty butt. Hopefully, I could wipe off with a few wet wipes, before for the doctor had to get all up in there and take a look around.

"Everything looks good," the doctor confirmed a little while later.

I didn't show any emotion.

"I know you asked about options. If you choose to go in that direction, the sooner, the better."

In the back of my mind, I'd known a long time ago, that I wouldn't be able to get rid of the baby. I didn't want it. That was me being honest with myself. But I knew that I couldn't kill it.

I told the doctor that I was going to keep it, and then after a little more chatting, he scheduled my next doctor's appointment, and I headed towards the exit sign.

I was smiling from ear to ear, and then…

Wait.

Is that?

Behind me, I heard *her* voice.

Satin.

I turned around just in time to see her going into the ultrasound room.

My heart dropped into the pit of my stomach.

She's pregnant?

What!

NO!

I tried to calm myself down. My skin burned, with fury, and I started to walk towards her voice.

And then they closed the door.

A nurse stopped me and asked me if I was okay.

I ignored her, and turned back around, looking for the exit, and then I started to run...literally.

I ran out of the building and all the way to my car.

The breeze smacked me in the face, and somehow my chest felt as though it was about to explode.

Satin was pregnant.

If she'd gone into that room, the same room that I'd been in plenty of times before, she was pregnant!

Oh God!

I was going to kill him!

Thea had talked me out of thinking crazy, that night, when I told her that I wanted West or Satin dead. She'd said that there was a better way to handle it all. She reminded me that I had five kids, that needed their mother.

Blah. Blah. Blah. Blah. Blah!

That's what her words sounded like in my head.

Somebody, if she was pregnant by my husband, was already, as good as dead!

Finally, I pulled myself together, enough to drive. I turned a twenty-minute drive home, into ten.

When I arrived, West's jeep was gone, and my mother's van was there.

"Where did he go?" I asked her immediately.

She shrugged. "All I know is that he asked me to come and watch them. He'd said that it was an emergency."

An emergency?

My head started to spin.

Was he going to the doctor with her?

I hadn't seen him, but that didn't mean that he hadn't been there or on his way.

If he was there with her, and didn't go with me...

Without saying another word to my mother, I ran back out of the front door. I sped back to the doctor's office. From what I could see, his car wasn't there, but I got out of the car and went back inside anyway.

"Mrs. Mason, is something wrong?"

"Uh, I think I forgot my phone back there."

"Hold on. I'll get someone to check for you."

"No. It's okay. I can go back there and look."

"I'm sorry, we don't allow patients back, unless they have an appointment scheduled. Or unless you're with someone who has an appointment."

She walked away from the desk. I was trying to see if Satin was still there.

A few minutes passed, and I'd only waited around, just in case Satin came out, because the more I thought about it, I knew that West couldn't be there with her.

I'd been going there, with all of my kids, so they knew that he was my husband.

I exhaled.

I'd wasted my time. I hadn't been thinking clearly.

West wasn't there.

"I'm sorry, but no one has seen a lost phone."

I turned away from her and headed back to the parking lot. I drove around and around, trying to remember exactly what type of car Satin had. I remembered the color, but I couldn't be sure if I saw it or not.

I was going to leave her ass sitting on four flat tires, but not wanting to make a mistake, and mess up the wrong car, I gave up on the idea, and drove away.

I called West.

He didn't answer, so I called the fire station.

No one answered the phone, so that meant that they were probably out.

When West didn't answer for a second time, curiosity forced me to drive by the fire station.

I exhaled, once I saw that West's jeep was there.

It was a work emergency.

Why hadn't he just said that?

I kept driving, but I was still thinking about Satin.

If she was having a baby; most likely, it was West's baby.

And on the life of my unborn child, there was no way in hell that I was going to let that happen!

I didn't care what I had to do, I had to stop it.

I had to stop her from having a baby with my husband.

But how?

~***~

"Are you still seeing her?"

West breathed hard, loud. "I'm trying to fix it."

"What do you mean, you're trying to fix it?"

"I'm trying to handle things, okay? But I don't feel like having this conversation with you every day!"

He yelled so loud that the kids peeked out of their rooms.

"I don't ask you every day."

"Yes, you do! It's the same damn thing, the same damn questions, every fucking day!"

I shrugged.

"So, what if I do?"

West veins started to show. "Like I said, I'm trying. Why are we talking about this? You don't need to be getting upset. Just let it go, Lava."

"Trying to what? Huh? Trying to what? Obviously, you're not trying hard enough."

West didn't reply.

"Tell me something, is she pregnant?"

He looked at me.

"What?"

"You heard me. Is she pregnant?"

"No."

"Are you sure about that?"

He glared at me. "What? Why? What are you trying to say Lava? How do you figure something like that, huh?"

I stood to my feet. "If that bitch pops up pregnant, with your baby, I swear to God I will make your life a living hell! I'll never accept that baby! And you won't even close to mine!"

"Is it even mine?" West asked and immediately he started to shake his head.

What?

What was he talking about?

What did he know?

"Are you seriously questioning whether or not me, your wife, is pregnant with your baby?"

He grabbed his keys.

"Hell, you never know."

He walked out of the house.

Something didn't sit right with me.

It was something about the way that he'd said it.

West drove away, and immediately, I called Thea and Tokyo.

"Neither of you have mentioned Kemp to anyone...have you? Anyone that might know West?"

Both of them said no.

"Why?" Thea asked.

"He just questioned if the baby was his."

"Really? Why!" Tokyo screamed.

"That's what I'm trying to figure out. He brushed it off like it was a general question, but the look on his face was like he knew something."

"Well, there's nothing to know. You're not seeing Kemp anymore. The baby IS his, so let him think what he wants to think," Tokyo said.

I was quiet for a moment.

And then I decided to tell them about Satin.

"I saw Satin the other day. At the doctor's office."

"And…" Thea asked.

"And I'm pretty sure that she's pregnant."

The ladies gasped in unison.

"He'd better hope and pray that if she is, that she's messing around with someone else too. I swear to God if she's pregnant by him, I'm going to lose it!"

The girls chatted back and forth for a while.

"Well, if she is and I hope not, but if she is pregnant by West, what is there to do?" Tokyo asked.

I thought long and hard about my response.

"There would be only one thing to do. Get rid of her and that damn baby…for good!"

"And how are you going to do that?" Tokyo wanted to know.

"I don't know. But I promise you, I will think of something."

~***~

"Ay, Bitch! Give me your purse!"

The man pointed something at my back.

"Okay. Okay. Here," I said reaching it to him.

It was late.

I'd been craving ice cream and since I'd cursed West out, he refused to go to the store and get me some.

So, I'd gone out to get the ice cream myself.

The man snatched my purse from my hands, and next thing I know, instead of just taking it and running away, he pushed me.

Hard.

As I hit the ground, the tub of ice cream slammed to the ground beside of me, and small amounts of the cold contents splattered all over my face.

Immediately, I could taste the blood from my lip.

My right elbow was throbbing, my knee burned with pain, and it felt extremely heavy.

And then I felt it.

The pain. The pain in my stomach.

"Help!" I somewhat whispered. And then I heard chatting heading in my direction, so with all of my might, I let out a scream.

"Help!"

"Unfortunately, Mrs. Mason, you lost the baby," the doctor at the hospital informed us.

West started to curse, and I just looked away.

"Your right arm is badly bruised, but nothing is broken. You sprang your wrist. And your knee is going to need stitches. I'm going to give you something for the pain."

West tried to hold my hand, but I snatched it away from him.

"I'm so sorry this happened to you."

I wasn't sure if I was sad, or mad, or relieved.

I was pretty sure that I was a combination of all of them, but clearly, West was more upset and heartbroken about the news than I was.

Evilly, I decided to add a little insult to his injury.

"This is all your fault. If you'd gone to get the ice cream, this would've never happened. It's your fault that our baby is dead," I said, and turned my head away from him.

West didn't say a word, but he stayed right there.

And never once left the room.

~***~

"Mama, you can go home. I'll be fine."

"Nonsense. Your father and I are going to stay here, and help you out, until West gets home from work.

I cringed at the sound of his name.

I didn't expect him to stay home with me after losing the baby. The only thing he loved more than me, *and* his mistress, was his position.

A position that I'd helped him to receive.

Being a firefighter was all that he knew.

He'd taken after his father, who had retired as a fire chief, many, many, years before West got into the game. He loved his job. He loved saving people. I wasn't sure if he liked the thrill of it all or if he just liked being labeled as a hero.

Either way, getting the job as the fire chief was so important to him.

He'd wanted it so badly.

The other guy that he was up against, had more experience. But West had more heart. More drive. And everything in me believed that West deserved that job.

I also had a feeling that he wasn't going to get it. I knew that it would destroy him, so I mentioned the job to Thea, and she suggested that we take matters into our own hands.

And so, we did.

It was all Thea's idea, but surprisingly, West hadn't tried to stop us.

Long story short, we set the Mayor's house on fire.

Virginia's Mayor lived only a block away from the fire station that West was stationed at, at the time.

What better way to get ahead of the competition, than to rescue the Mayor from a fire?

West knew that they would get the call.

He'd said that he would be up and that he would be ready. He would be waiting for us to carry out our plan. West figured that he would get there in time, and after saving the Mayor, he would have the job in the bag.

So, we set Thea's crazy plan into motion.

In all black, late at night, with Thea by my side, we worked as a team and started a fire around the Mayor's house and just as the flames started to grow, Thea and I ran away.

Needless to say, things almost turned bad.

West told us to start a big enough fire for rescue, but not so big to where the Mayor and his wife would be in real danger. He'd said to start the fire towards the back of the house, but Thea hadn't listened.

She'd gotten a little too happy with the gasoline, and West actually ended up having to earn that position by going in, and saving the Mayor, his wife, as well as their trapped six-year-old, grand-daughter, who we hadn't known was inside. She was severely burned, and it was all our fault, but thankfully, she didn't die.

West saved her.

The Mayor was extremely thankful. He raved about West, to the newspapers, and all over T.V. The whole state called West a hero. And just like that, the other guy was out of the running, and West had the job of his dreams.

All because of Thea and me.

"It's okay to be sad, you know."

"I know." I frowned. "I'm just trying to figure out what it is that I need to do."

Mama stood up from the edge of the bed.

"You do whatever you need to do to save your marriage," is all that she said, and then she left me alone to try to figure out what she meant.

The baby was gone, so what little hope there was for West and I was probably gone too. He'd probably only been attempting to be around because I'd been pregnant. And now that I wasn't, I was sure that things were going to go back to how they were before.

And then I remembered.

Satin was still pregnant.

West had to know that all of this time, I was bluffing about turning him in for the fire. I mean, I'd helped, and so had Thea, so if he went down, so did we.

It was only a matter of time, before he realized that, and once he did, he wouldn't care about my threats and nothing would stop him from walking out of that front door one day, and never coming back.

And if she was pregnant by him, my guess was that it would be sooner, then later.

Maybe if he was cheating because I was a horrible wife, and had neglected his needs, I could understand that. Hell, even if he'd simply asked me for a divorce, two years ago, instead of asking me to allow him to cheat.

I would've been hurt, and upset, but I probably would've accepted it, eventually, and given it to him.

But knowing that he would be leaving me, to be with someone, who I've shared that last two years of my marriage with, someone who looked the way that she did, someone who had been so much more of a woman that she could take my husband away from me, and on top of that, had the nerve to get pregnant by him…

It was unacceptable!

She could never have him.

And he couldn't have her.

"Hey, are you hungry?"

My mother stuck her head into my bedroom.

I shook my head.

"You sure? I got some of those peanuts that you like."

Peanuts?

I thought back to my last conversation with Kemp.

He'd said that Satin was allergic to peanuts.

I shook my head at my mother, and once she walked away, I reached for my phone.

"Google, can you have a miscarriage if you have an allergic reaction?"

I spoke into the mic of my phone, and anxiously, I waited for the results to appear.

~***~

I screwed on the lid of the small tube, filled with peanut oil, and placed it in the side of my bra.

I pushed the big bottle of oil, back to the back of the cabinet, where it had been for quite some time.

There were a few cases where allergic reactions, had led to a miscarriage, and I was hoping that would be the case tonight.

Of course, there were tons of cases, where it could lead to death. Kemp had stated that she'd almost died, once before, and though surprisingly, I wasn't trying to kill Satin, this time, I was hoping that just a small drop, would cause a reaction, that was bad enough to make her lose her child.

That's if she was really pregnant.

With the pregnancy out of the picture, we would be on an even playing field, again, and this time, I was prepared to actually put up a fight.

I just had to get rid of her leverage first.

I was surprised that I was actually going to go through with it all, but there was no stopping me, especially since West hadn't come home in four days.

He would answer when I called him, sometimes, but he would never tell me where he was. We would argue, and he would only say that he needed space and then he would hang up in my face.

He?

Needed space?

I'd just been attacked, robbed, and lost a baby, but he needed space?

My anger towards him, fueled my rage. I felt as though I hadn't slept in days. West and Satin were always on my mind and I hated not knowing where she lived.

She'd changed her number, from the one that was on her résumé. I'd tried calling it, once West had been gone for two days, only to find that it was disconnected.

I'd gone by the fire station, but West wouldn't let me in. They'd all just let me stand out there, knocking, kicking and screaming, but no one would come to the door.

I was going crazy

And then…there was light.

Kemp.

I'd given in and called him, to try and get just the slightest idea of where his sister lived. I hadn't thought it all the way through, but luckily, I hadn't had to.

Kemp said that he missed me, and then he asked me to meet him at the bar.

He'd said that it was birthday, and that some of his family and friends, were gathering there to celebrate.

Surely that meant that his sister was going to be in attendance.

Perfect.

That would probably be my only chance of getting close to Satin. My only chance to find out for sure if she was pregnant, and my only chance to do something about it.

And I was going to take it!

"Y'all ready?"

I walked into the living room.

Thea and Tokyo were waiting for me.

I'd told them about the baby, and my plan.

I knew that if Satin was pregnant, she wouldn't be drinking, but maybe she would have a water, or something that I could slip a little bit of the peanut oil into.

It wouldn't take much.

My second child, Lonnie, was allergic to lemons, strangely, and if just a tip of lemon juice, so much as got into her mouth, we had to get her the proper care immediately.

Just a drip.

Maybe she would start choking and fall to the ground, hard enough to cause a miscarriage.

It was wrong.

Dead wrong.

Someone had just taken my child from me. And here I was, planning to do the same to her.

But this was her own fault.

She brought this on herself. She had no business sleeping with someone else's husband. I'd made up in my mind, that one way or another, I was getting my husband back. And if she wasn't going to give him back to me, well...

I was just going to have to take him.

"Let's do this," Thea said. "And if this little plan doesn't work, or if you don't get close enough, to slip that oil into her drink, I'm just going to push her down. My "push down game" is strong! You better ask about me! Hell, we can go in and do things my way, from the start. Problem solved."

"Thea, I swear you will do, and say anything," Tokyo laughed.

"You have no idea," Thea mumbled.

"Honestly, Lava, do you think that this is…"

"If you're going to say something logical Tokyo, I don't want to hear it. You have the heart of gold. We know that. And once upon a time, I did too. But that didn't get me anywhere, and right now, all I want to do is be angry. All I want to do is be crazy. Is that okay?" I asked her.

Tokyo looked sad. "Okay."

We headed out, and the whole car ride, none of us said a word. I figured that we were all thinking about the same thing.

I hoped that West was with her.

I wanted to embarrass them, in a bar full of people. I wanted to expose her for the whore that she was. And I wanted to make the beloved Fire Chief, look like shit too.

We walked into the bar, and immediately, I spotted Kemp.

He was wearing a black and red blazer, a bow-tie, and I was sure that he'd worn his hair up in a ponytail on purpose.

He knew that it turned me on.

"The only birthday present I need," he whispered, once he was close enough to me. "All I needed was to see you."

He eyed me, somewhat sexually, and I pretended to be interested, but I wasn't.

I looked past him.

I was looking at his sister.

Someone called Kemp's name and he told me that he would catch up to me later.

My heart was racing, as we neared the bar. Thea elbowed me, and turned her back towards Satin's direction, just in case she remembered her from slapping her.

"Oh my god, what do you know. I just keep running into you," I allowed Satin to notice me.

I was frustrated that West had never shown her a picture of his wife. That she still didn't have the slightest clue as to who I really was.

"Do you come here often?" I made conversation with her.

"Yes. It's my family's place."

I eyed her cup.

"Is that a mixed drink? What kind? I love to try new drinks."

She smiled.

"Oh no. It's just cranberry juice. I'm pregnant!" She squealed.

I had to cough to keep from calling her all kinds of bitches and stuff.

"Congratulations. How far along are you?"

"Only a few months. It's taking forever for me to show. I'm so excited!"

She was glowing.

I wanted to stab her.

"Is the father excited, as well?"

"Oh, yes! Girl, he's ecstatic! All he…"

She didn't get to finish her sentence. Someone approached her and started to talk to her.

I rolled my eyes as I slowly, turned away from her and grabbed the tiny bottle out of my bra. Turning towards the bar, with my hands low, I unscrewed the lid.

"What can I get for you?" The bartender said out of nowhere, scaring me half to death.

"A double shot of Hennessey," I said to him. He nodded.

I turned my attention back to Satin.

She was still talking. Her drink was in her hand, as she rested her back up against the bar.

I waited for her to either sit the cup down or move it to where I could get closer to it.

It seemed as though the longer I held the bottle, and thought about what I was about to do, the more and more, I started to change my mind.

This is ridiculous Lava. This is too far. It's just too much.

My mind and my heart seemed to be at a tug-a-war.

This isn't me.

I was a hardworking wife and mother. I was kind and caring. I wasn't a baby killer. I wasn't some crazy person.

I was normal. I wasn't as heartless as Thea.

Right then and there, I told myself to walk away, but my feet wouldn't move. Then, I told myself that if an opportunity didn't present itself, then Monday morning, I was just going to sit my pride aside, and go to the courthouse and file for a divorce.

I was just going to give up and let it be.

Just as the thought crossed my mind, Satin threw her head back as she laughed, and for a second, I was so caught up in how beautiful she was in the dim light, that I almost didn't notice that she was taking a sip of the drink. She took a piece of whatever it was that her friend was eating, ate it, and then took another sip.

She swallowed and then placed the cup down at her side.

Perfect.

I inched closer to her, almost shoulder to shoulder.

I put the lid in my pouch as I took out a $10 bill, because I spotted the bartender heading in my direction.

"Thank you. Keep the change."

Hastily, nervously, I grabbed the drink with one hand and placed the tube of peanut oil over her drink with the other.

I tried to concentrate. I moved slowly, only trying to drop a single drip into her cup.

"Excuse me!"

My heart dropped.

A man had bumped into me, in a hurry to get to the bar, causing me to almost drop my drink, and messing up my concentration on pouring to oil.

"Damn, watch where you're going!" Thea screamed at the drunk man, that was now in between us.

Terrified, I started to walk away.

"Hey. Sorry! It was nice running into you!" Satin shouted behind me. I turned around to nod at her and caught her taking a sip of the drink.

"Let's go. Let's go. Let's go!" I mumbled, walking past Thea and Tokyo.

I rushed for the door.

"Ay. Ay Ay. Leaving so soon?"

"Yes. I got a call. My son has a fever," I lied.

Kemp nodded.

"Okay, was all that he said, as I pushed the doors of the bar open.

I walked fast, with my head down, until I reached the car. I didn't notice that I still had the drink in my hand until I stopped. Hurriedly, I downed it.

"What happened? Did you do it?" Thea whispered, immediately, once she caught up to me.

"Unlock the doors," I said to her, without answering her question.

Once inside of the car, for the first time, I looked at the small tube of peanut oil. Thea and Tokyo looked at it too. And then we looked at each other.

Half of the bottle was…empty.

~***~

The young woman, who apparently had some kind of allergic reaction at the "Purple Cocaine" bar last night, has died. She collapsed last night, unable to breathe. And was immediately rushed to the hospital. It is said that she had an allergic reaction to peanuts. They are still trying to pin point the source of the food or drink that caused the reaction to occur. No foul play is expected, as of yet.

She died?

Almost losing my balance, I grabbed a hold of the arm of the chair and sat down.

Satin was dead.

I tried to sort through my feelings, but all I found was regret.

What have I done?

Sorrow consumed me, and then fear and worry took its place.

What if it comes back to me?

What if someone saw me?

Jail.

Prison.

I would lose everything. Not just West; I would lose my life. My job. My kids.

It was too much. I'd poured too much. But I didn't mean to. It wasn't my fault. It was an accident. The drunk man bumped me. I was only going to pour a drip.

Who would believe me?

What was I thinking?

Why hadn't someone stopped me?

Why hadn't Thea, or Tokyo, tried to stop me?

I felt as guilty as a pastor, buying a new Benz, with the church members money.

I placed my head in my hands and tried to focus on taking deep breaths. Somehow, my breathing turned into panting, and then my panting was replaced by crying.

I killed someone.

I killed her.

I killed my husband's mistress.

And even though no foul play was suspected, as of yet, what if they found something?

I saw my life flash before my eyes, and in the midst of crying, what seemed like a pool full of tears, I heard the front door open.

Sniffling, I lifted up my head.

After five days of not being home, he shows up after his mistress is dead.

West.

****

Chapter Five

I stared at him.

I couldn't believe that he hadn't said anything.

About her. Or about her death.

He was acting normal.

As though she wasn't dead. As though he hadn't lost her. As though he didn't care.

He'd told me, out of his own mouth that he loved her.

He had to be hurting.

Was he putting on a show?

West walked in a few days ago, catching me in tears.

He'd asked me what was wrong. I hadn't known how to answer him, so I just sat there, and then he sat down in front of me.

And then he started to talk.

He talked about himself. He talked about us. But never about her. Never about Satin, or the baby, or the fact that she had died.

He'd said that he missed the kids, and until we figured out what was next, for us, he would be coming back home.

That was it.

That was all that he'd said.

"Your phone is ringing again."

I was avoiding Thea and Tokyo.

They had to know by now that Satin was dead, and I didn't know what to say to them.

I glanced at my phone, but surprisingly, it wasn't either of them.

It was Kemp.

Oh Kemp.

I hadn't thought of him, in all of this. Not once had he crossed my mind, as to how he might be handling Satin's death.

I picked up my phone and grabbed my purse and keys.

"Oh. That must be your new man," West mumbled.

"I'm just trying to be like you," I slammed the front door behind me.

I hopped into my car, just as Kemp started to call again.

"Hello?"

"I need to see you."

"What's wrong?"

He was quiet. "Haven't you watched the news?"

"No," I lied.

Kemp was quiet for a while, and then he repeated his statement. "I need to see you."

I owed him that much, right?

After what I'd done.

Without thinking too much about it, I headed in his direction.

As soon as I hung up the phone, Thea called again.

"Don't be ignoring me!"

"I'm sorry. I…"

"I know. Remember. I know. But don't shut me out. I'm here for you. We all know that her dying, wasn't the plan."

"It never should've been *a* plan in the first place. What the hell was I thinking Thea?"

"You were thinking with a broken heart. And a broken heart doesn't fight fair. A broken heart doesn't play by the rules."

I was silent. And then I started to whine.

"Thea, I'm going to lose everything. I'm going to go to jail and lose my kids."

"The news said that they aren't suspecting any foul play."

"For now."

We listened to each other breathe for a while, and then finally, Thea spoke. "I love you. And everything is going to be okay. Hopefully."

"Hopefully?"

"Ying and I are going out of the country for a while."

"What? When did y'all decide this?"

"Something came up."

"Something like what?"

Thea ignored my question. "I'll call you when we get settled. Try not to worry too much. Everything is going to be fine."

She hung up.

Briefly, I wondered what was going on with her and Ying. It had to be something sudden, otherwise, Thea would've told me if they had plans to travel, a long time ago.

I tried calling her back, but she didn't answer.

So, I left her a voicemail, just as I arrived at Kemp's house.

He was sitting on the front porch, as though he'd been waiting for me.

I took a deep breath and checked my face.

Slowly, I got out of the car and walked towards him.

"My sister died."

I didn't know what I was supposed to say or do, so I pretended to be shocked.

"Oh my God, no. I'm so sorry."

I inched closer to him and took a seat at his side.

"I leave for Egypt in the morning. She's being buried there. In our traditional style."

They were taking her body to Egypt?

Did that mean that there wasn't going to be an investigation of her death? Did that mean that I really was off the hook?

Had I gotten away with murder?

"How did she die?"

"She had an allergic reaction...to peanuts," he looked at me. "Why didn't you tell me that you knew her?"

I looked as though I was confused.

"I watched the footage from that night and I saw you speaking to her."

Footage?

It hadn't crossed my mind that there might be cameras inside of the bar.

Immediately, I became nervous. I was as nervous as a nun in a strip club, and I knew that Kemp could tell.

"I...I...didn't know her. I overheard her say that she was your sister. So, I made conversation."

Kemp stared at me.

"Now, with her gone, everything is on me, and when my folks are gone, everything that we've built, will be mine. Just as it should be. I'm the one who made our family fortune possible, in the first place, because of my marriage. Still, somehow, she'd always had the spotlight."

I couldn't tell if it was sadness in his voice, or liberation. And then, for the first time, I realized that Kemp was jealous.

He'd been jealous of Satin, all of this time.

"Thank you," he said to me.

"For what? Coming over? You sounded like you needed me."

Kemp shook his head.

"No. Thank you…for what you did."

What?

I touched my chest.

"I…What…"

"Like I said. I watched the tape."

The tips of my fingers started to tingle for some odd reason, as I stuttered.

"It was obvious that you were doing something with your hands. So, I zoomed in on the video. And I knew that I'd mentioned her peanut allergy to you."

I didn't know what to say. I didn't want to admit to it, but I knew that I couldn't deny it.

"I told the police that there wasn't a tape. I told them that she had a habit of eating things that she wasn't supposed to and that maybe she'd tasted something, from someone, not knowing its ingredients."

"So...you're...not...that's it?"

"That's it." Kemp stood up.

I sat there in shock.

"As I told you. I'm not a good man. I have plenty of secrets of my own. My own sins to answer to. And now you have yours."

"But...but...she was your sister."

"I know. Luckily for you, she made my life a living hell."

Surprised by his comments, finally, I stood up.

"You hated her. That much?"

"If your sister was responsible for the death of your wife and child, you would hate her too."

My mouth opened wide.

He'd never told me that.

"I thought you said that you were divorced and that your wife moved away."

"I lied. It was a cover-up. For Satin. Years ago, my wife had gone out with Satin one night, unaware that she was pregnant. Satin was driving drunk, and there was an accident. My wife died. Satin lived. My father knew a few people, who knew a few other people, and just like that, it was as though it'd never even happened. And Satin went unpunished."

He waited on me to say something, but I didn't.

"It's just easier for me to say that I'm divorced."

I was distraught.

It wasn't jealousy, at all. It was hatred.

He'd hated Satin even more than I had.

I guess you just never know what truth someone is hiding; even when you think that you've asked them all of the right questions.

Kemp looked at me, for a long time, as though he was trying to remember every curve of my face. Finally, he started to walk away. And then suddenly, he stopped and turned around. "Let me guess, she...your husband...need I say more?"

I nodded.

He scoffed. "She was always trying to find love on her own. The only problem was, that the love that she found, usually belonged to someone else." He shook his head. "I'll be staying in Egypt, after the burial, for a long, long while. So, this is, goodbye Lava. For real. Forever. I'll never forget that beautiful face of yours, or that smile. And that laugh. Yeah. Your laugh is something special."

Kemp walked closer to me and then he kissed me. He kissed me hard, and full of regret. His lips and tongue assured me, that he was leaving for good…forever.

After a few minutes, finally, he pulled away from me.

"For your sake, I hope your sin was worth it. Not all of mine were," and with that, Kemp walked inside of his house, and closed his front door, never looking back at me again.

~***~

"What do you mean?"

I was talking to Thea and Tokyo on three-way.

"He isn't saying anything. He's acting as though nothing happened. As though she isn't dead. At least to me. Maybe he's venting to other people about it, like his friend George. He called him the other day, like ten times. West would answer the phone, and then disappear out of the room, or even go outside for a while. And he's constantly texting, but it's just weird. He doesn't seem sad at all."

I hadn't been able to sleep. I hadn't been able to eat. I still hadn't gone back to work. I was an emotional wreck.

Even though Satin's body was gone, and no one was looking for me, living with the guilt of what I'd done was eating me up inside.

"Does he even know, that you know, that she's dead?" Thea asked.

"I haven't mentioned anything to him. I haven't said anything at all because I'm scared that I might cry. I feel…"

"Put your feelings in your back pocket, Lava. You weren't trying to kill her. It was an accident."

Doesn't make it right.

"Have you spoken to Kemp?" Tokyo asked.

Briefly, I filled them in on my meeting with Kemp. I told them that we were truly over and that he was moving away. I also said that he was sad about Satin's death. I didn't tell them about his truth or about the tape, or that he knew what I'd done.

"Well, at least it's over. There's no case. No issues. They suspected no foul play. All that you can do now is try to forget what you've done. Lord knows, I tried to," Thea said.

"Where are you anyway?" Tokyo asked her.

"China. So, a cop showed up, at our house, on the day that we left. He asked me about my step-father's death.

After all of these years. I told him that I didn't know the man that killed him, and the cop said that they'd had some kind of anonymous tip, to come in, saying that someone also seen a woman near the scene that night. The case, of course, has never been solved, and he wanted to know if I knew of anyone that could've wanted him dead. He never came right out and ask me, but he was looking at me funny. As though he was leaving something out, and like there was something that he wasn't telling me. But I played it cool, and finally, he left. And then, that same exact day, another cop shows up, a different one, saying that they needed to ask Ying some questions. Something about money laundering or something. I told him that he should've been at work, even though I knew that he wasn't. As soon as he left, I called Ying and asked him about it."

"And what did he say?"

"He said…Hell Yeah!"

I laughed on accident.

"So, he was laundering money?" Tokyo sounded appalled.

"I don't know all of the details. All I know is that he did know a little too much information about some offshore accounts and whatever the hell else he started to blab about. So, I told him to meet me at the airport. I took everything out of our safe, somehow Ying moved all of our money, from our accounts, to somewhere else, and just like that, we were China bound."

"But you're not staying there, right? What the hell would I do without you?"

"Well, Ying has a plan to clear his name, and hopefully the questions, about my perverted stepdaddy's death, would have disappeared by the time that we get back. If not, then…home girl, you better learn how to speak Chinese or something, and come and visit. If we haven't packed up and gone somewhere else by then."

Thea laughed, but I knew that she was serious.

She said that she had to go, and left Tokyo and I to have a conversation.

"Everyone is asking about you at work. It just isn't the same without you here."

"I'm pretty sure that Edgar hasn't asked about me. I'm sure that he thinks that he runs the place now, don't he?"

"Girl, yes. But he asked me out."

"I knew it! I knew that he had a thing for you! I told you that, didn't I? I told you!"

"Yeah. You did. And I don't know. The divorce is final, but I think that I just want a break. A break from loving anybody, other than myself. Men are too inconsistent. One day they love you. The next day they don't. That shit is stressful."

"Honey, you don't have to tell me. Hopefully, I can get some kind of handle on my situation."

"You will," she encouraged me.

We spoke a while longer, and I told her that I had to go, once George, West's friend, beeped in.

"Hello?" I answered.

"Lava! Come quick! There's been an accident! It's West!"

I dropped my phone and clutched my chest.

~***~

"Do you need anything?"

"I'm fine."

West almost died in a fire.

There was a bomb that had gone off at the court house. The building was still burning, that day once I got to the scene.

It was complete chaos.

Thirty people; including two federal judges and a hand full of officers died. They were calling it some kind of terrorist attack, but they didn't know who was responsible for it as of yet.

I was so thankful that my sister, Drea, hadn't been in court that day, or the situation would've been worse, than it already was.

West had been there, doing his job, trying to save as many people as possible. In the process of saving a female officer, parts of the roof started to cave in. His left leg was badly crushed, and he'd inhaled a good amount of smoke. About 25% of the right-side of his body was burned, before the other firefighters, found a way to get to him and pulled him out. The female officer that he'd been trying to save, didn't make it, but somehow, he did.

His right arm and hand were burned pretty badly. Luckily, he was still able to move and use them, but it was going to take a long while for him to heal. The other burns were minor and a lot less severe. He'd had to have immediate surgery on his leg, and although he had to get a few screws inside of it, they were expecting him to regain full use of it.

"While I was lying there, all I could think about was you. And the kids. But especially you. I kept seeing your smile, and visions of you in your wedding gown. I could hear your laugh. I could smell the scent of your skin. Your voice was like a sweet melody in my ear. It's amazing that though death was staring me in the face, all I could do was smile, because all I could see in my darkest moment, was you."

My heart fluttered.

West hadn't said anything like that to me in a very long time.

"I know I've messed up. I know I don't deserve you. Or a second chance. But I want one. I'll heal. I'll be back at work soon. But until then, I want to spend every single day, trying to make you fall in love with me again. I will never, ever, hurt you again Lava. You'll never have to worry about another woman again. I promise."

Yeah, because she's dead.

I kept telling myself that it wasn't intentional.

That the man bumped me, causing me to pour too much peanut oil into her cup. I told myself that killing her wasn't the plan. Just her baby, which was just as bad, if not worse.

I should've never gone there that night.

The thoughts should've never crossed my mind.

Often, I wondered if she could taste the difference in her drink. Cranberry juice is fairly strong, but I wondered if she'd noticed the taste and spit it out as soon as she did.

Or had she drunk the whole cup?

Maybe, just that one sip, that I'd seen her take, caused the reaction, and she just hadn't been as lucky as she was the time before.

Either way, I was responsible.

And here he was, acting as though he'd ended things voluntarily. I wasn't sure of what kind of game he was trying to play, but I realized something, the day of the bombing, when I thought that he was going to die.

I realized that I didn't hate him as much as I thought I did. In fact, I was still very much in love with him.

"If you want a divorce…" I started.

"I don't. I want you."

"You're just in shock."

"No. I'm just in awe. I'm in awe that I forgot the type of woman that I was married to. That I forgot how much you mean to me. Maybe it took me almost dying to see it, but I see it. I see you." Though the words coming out of his mouth were sweet, the look on his face told me that he was in pain, so I ended the conversation and made sure that he was comfortable in bed.

His phone was ringing over and over again.

Who is that?

It couldn't be Satin. She was dead.

After about the tenth call, he looked at me, and then looked at it. Usually, he guarded his phone with his life, but West did something new and turned the screen of his phone in my direction.

"It's just George. See."

Yeah. It was.

Again…

~***~

"I can't believe that you're back at work," Tokyo said.

"Well, with West down, one of us needs to go to work. We have five mouths to feed. Besides, I'm feeling a little better."

She noticed my smile.

"Uh oh. What happened?"

"I'm not sure yet. West wants to work things out. After all that we've been through. After what I've done," I whispered. "And after he almost died. I just can't believe…"

"That things actually look like they're going to get better?"

I nodded. "Yeah."

West and I were in a weird space.

He was complimenting me, and constantly begging for my forgiveness. And if I was being truthful, I was overwhelmed. Though I'd wanted him back, at least I thought I did, now, that I had him, more or less, I still resented him.

I was sure that it was because of what I'd done. I couldn't help but to wonder if he'd even be interested in working things out if Satin was still alive.

I still had so many unanswered questions, tons of mixed feelings, and a new lingering suspicion.

Why in the hell was his friend George calling him so much?

He called him all day, every day. Sure, they were close, and worked together, but damn!

I got the feeling that there was something wrong, but what could it be?

"Well, I'm going out with Edgar," she laughed.

"Girl, I can't wait to hear what happens…"

I halted my sentence, once our boss came into my office.

Harris worked upstairs. I never saw him. He never came down…unless it was important.

"Can I speak to you for a minute?"

Tokyo greeted him, politely, and then she hurried out of my office, closing the door behind her.

"Hey. I know I've been gone…"

"There's no easy way to say this, but something has come to my attention, that I have to address. A little while ago, I received a phone call from a lady that you interviewed, Satin Gamal."

My heart skipped a beat, at the mention of her name.

"Apparently, you used her information from her résumé to stalk her."

What?

I opened my mouth, but he continued.

"She called in, a long while ago, to report that after interviewing her, you'd been following her."

She knew?

But how?

Did that mean that she'd known who I was the whole time?

"You have been out of work for quite some time, so I never got the chance to address it. I saw on the news that she's passed away since then, but either way, I don't condone that type of behavior. Your actions were unacceptable. I don't know why you were following her and I don't care. Effective immediately, Lava, you're fired."

"But…"

He walked out of the office, without giving me a chance to explain.

In shock, I just sat there for a long time, unable to move.

How did she know that I was following her?

Did she see me in the car that day, the day that Thea slapped her?

Or had she known that I was West's wife all along?

Why didn't she say anything?

Without grabbing anything but my purse, embarrassed, I rushed out of the building, brokenhearted.

Though I had been going through a lot, lately, I loved my job. I loved the people and what the organization stood for. I'd planned on staying there, forever, and now my job was yet another thing that I'd lost, along with my dignity, my sanity, my innocence, and my respect, all because of West.

I called Thea, but she didn't answer her phone, so after riding around for a whole hour, finally, I went home.

I walked into the house, in one hell of a bad mood.

"West?"

I headed to our bedroom. He was in the bathroom.

I took off my shoes, just as his phone started to ring.

George.

I answered it.

"Hello?"

I didn't hear anything.

"Hello? George?"

After a short pause, the phone hung up.

The bathroom door opened, and West seemed shocked to see me. He hopped on his good leg towards me, and immediately took his phone out of my hand.

"What are you doing home?"

"I got fired. Why has George been calling you like that? What's going on?"

"Fired? Why? What happened?"

"It's a long story." I folded my arms across my chest.

"Well, we have plenty of savings, and I'm getting the check for being out of work. You can stay home. Take a break. You can always find another job."

He sat on his side of the bed. I sat on mine.

"I asked you a question. Why is George calling you like crazy?"

West looked at me. "He's going through something."

"Something like what?"

He didn't say anything.

"See. But I'm supposed to be able to trust you, right?" I yelled at him and stood up.

168

West exhaled. "He lost someone that was important to him."

"Who? Cheyenne didn't die, did she?"

"No. It wasn't Cheyenne."

I caught on to the way that he'd said it. I huffed.

"Oh, let me guess, he was cheating on his wife too?"

West just looked at me again.

"Damn! Do all fire fighters cheat? I guess you all just do whatever the hell y'all want to do over there, huh? So, what, you were sleeping with Satin and he was…"

"What? I wasn't sleeping with Satin," West said.

For a moment, time stood still.

What?

"What did you say?"

"I wasn't sleeping with Satin."

"But…but…you told me that your mistress name was Satin."

He stood up. "Lava, I lied about her name. Satin was sleeping with George. That's why he's hurting. Because Satin died."

No! This couldn't be happening.

"Why would you lie about something like that? Why lie about her name?"

"Because Lava…I didn't see any point in telling you her name. But you kept asking, and asking…and asking, so that day, I just blurted out Satin to get you off of my back."

So, wait a minute…I'd killed the wrong woman?

"Satin was sleeping with George."

"Then who the hell are you sleeping with?"

"I'm not sleeping with anyone…anymore."

My head was spinning.

"But I saw you one night. At that bar. I was with Thea, riding by and I saw you, with Satin. You hugged her. I saw you walk into the bar with her."

"She and I had become good friends. I was the only one that knew about their affair. Her and George both used me as their person to vent to. If I hugged her, it was innocent. Strictly platonic. She'd become a friend. Wait, you saw me with her?"

I didn't respond to him.

"She was the one, that died at the bar, from an allergic reaction. The one that's been on the news. That was her. That was Satin."

I couldn't believe what he was saying to me.

That's why he wasn't sad.

That's why he hadn't mentioned it.

"And you knew what George was doing to Cheyenne? The whole time?"

"Her family owns that bar. We would see her there all the time. She would sit and chat with us, and then, her and George started this thing."

I was panting, as West stared at me with confusion, as to why I was so upset.

This was crazy!

She'd been sleeping with George the whole time.

Not West.

She'd been pregnant by George...not West!

Oh my God!

All of this time I was looking at the wrong woman. I was worried about the wrong girl.

Words couldn't describe what I felt at that moment.

"What's her name?" I asked him through clinched teeth.

"What?"

"Her name! Her *real* name! What's your mistress's name?" I screamed at him.

"It doesn't matter. We're over. That's all you need to know and worry about. I'm not seeing her anymore, Lava."

His phone started to ring again in his hand, and I could see that the name on the screen said George.

West hopped out of the room, and I just sat there.

Sad and in shock, I heard him open the front door.

Oh God.

This was crazy!

I'd killed the wrong whore!

****

Chapter Six

"Oh, he needs his ass whooped for that!" Thea screamed in my ear.

I'd just told her that Satin wasn't West's mistress and that all along, he'd been lying about her name.

Since I'd discovered the truth, most days, I didn't know whether I was coming or going. West and I were arguing again. We argued mostly about the real identity of his mistress. The curiosity was killing me. I wanted to know who she was.

"And he won't tell you who she is?"

"No. He says that it's over."

"Do you believe him."

"I don't know."

Thea attempted to get me to look at the bright side of the situation, but I couldn't see through the rain.

I'd thought that I had answers, only to find out that all along, I hadn't known anything at all.

"And after what I did, to the wrong woman, I can barely stand the sight of him!"

"I told you to take my approach from the very beginning! You should've approached her, and let her know that you are West's wife, after we saw them hug that night at the bar. That way, she could've told you right then and there, that she wasn't sleeping with your husband. She was sleeping with a different dog."

And now I couldn't do a thing to make it right.

Had she just had a fall or a miscarriage, she could've just tried again, but she would never get the chance to.

All because of me.

"I saw Ying on T.V."

"Yeah. Chile, they're looking for his ass."

"They're saying that he's responsible for millions of missing dollars."

"It ain't missing. He has it."

"And you're okay with that? With being on the run with him?"

"Girl, I'm ride or die. I ain't going no damn where. And besides, with all of the money that he took, they ain't ever going to find us. Until after Ying executes some little plan to clear his name, even though he *is* guilty. He says that he's going to link everything to someone else that is involved, that tried to turn it all on him, but he says that his plan will take time. And since I don't have anything better to do," Thea laughed. I didn't. "We're leaving China, knowing that they'll probably start looking here, eventually. You know, Ying's family and all. For a while, we're going to travel the world. Ying was prepared. He had a feeling that this day would come. Girl, he already had fake identities, a boat, a jet that I had no idea about, and there's no telling what else."

"Be careful Thea. I don't want you to end up in prison."

"I won't. If they catch his ass, I already told him that I'm going to tell them that he kept me hostage and forced me to go with him. He's cool with that. And as for my issue, I talked to Mama. She said the cops visited her too. She said once they started asking about me, she told him that he'd had a gambling problem and that a man from up North had been looking for him and threating to kill him for quite some time. Everybody knew that he liked to gamble, so, as far as they know, if they started asking other people, they may think that its true. She said that the officer told her that someone gave them a tip. A tip to look into me, as his killer, but she assured them that I could never do something like that. She didn't even ask me if I'd done it. Or if I'd had something to do with it. All she said was that she was sorry that she hadn't believed me about him, when I was younger."

I was still stuck on this random tip.

Who had saw Thea out there that night all of those years ago? Why had they come forward now?

Thea and I said our goodbyes, and she promised to call as often as she could. Still holding the phone to my ear, even after she hung up, I sat there, in deep thought and somehow, Kemp crossed my mind.

I'd always been able to talk to him. I wondered what he would say about West's lie. I wondered what he would do to find out that his sister's death was pointless; just as much as it was a mistake.

West wobbled into the room, with a frustrated look on his face.

"What's wrong?"

"Nothing."

I headed towards the knock on the door.

"Hello, Mrs. Lava Mason? We need to ask you some questions about Kemp? Kemp Gamal."

I looked behind me to see that West was standing there.

"You had a relationship with him correct?"

I didn't know what to say.

"Look, we know that you and Kemp were romantically involved. I'm not here to get into your marriage, but we do need to know, if you know, how to find him. We also have reason to believe that you may have known what he'd been planning."

I looked at him perplexed.

"Planning?"

"So, you knew nothing about the bomb?"

"Bomb? What bomb?"

"The bomb that almost killed your husband."

I looked back and forth between West and the officer.

"I have no idea what you're talking about."

"Kemp is believed to be the bombing suspect. He was spotted, disguised as a police officer that day. We're not sure where the bomb was placed or hidden, or how he as well as it, went unnoticed, but moments after he came out of the building, the bomb went off."

I thought that he was gone?

He was supposed to have left for Egypt.

"We found out that you were seeing him. We even have a few videos of the two of you being spotted together. We all know that pillow talk is a mother---." The officer cleared his throat. "I just need to know if you knew about the bomb. If he said anything. And if you know how to find him."

I was sweating bullets.

Was this his secret and sin that he'd been referring to?

Why he'd constantly said that he wasn't a good person? Because he was going to kill innocent people?

"I didn't know anything about a bomb. He and I were just…"

"Having sex?"

"Friends."

"With benefits? We found small things of yours still in the house that he was renting."

"Renting? He'd said that his ex-wife left him that house."

"I guess you didn't really know the man that you were sleeping with at all, did you? The house was a rental. Expensive. But he was renting it. And I'm pretty sure that Kemp Gamal isn't his real name."

Then had Satin Gamal been a fake name too?

"I don't know where he is. I didn't know about the bomb. And according to you, I didn't even know his real name. I have a number for him, but that's all that I have."

The officer asked me to get my cell phone and to call him.

"Put it on speaker."

Feeling embarrassed, I pressed on his number and placed it on speaker phone.

The number you have reached has been disconnected.

"Figures." The officer said. "Well, if he contacts you, or if you can think of anything, give me a call," he said, reaching me his card.

He spoke to West, as if they were well acquainted, and then finally he was gone.

For a long while, neither West, nor I said a word. Finally, he broke his silence.

"Of all of the people, you go out and have a goddamn affair with a terrorist!"

He screamed loudly.

"You're one to judge! You drove me into another man's arms! And for the record, I didn't know that he was a terrorist. He was kind, and genuine, and...like I said, I didn't know."

I couldn't believe it.

Someone as sweet, and subtle as Kemp, had planned to bomb and kill innocent people? All along?

I didn't know who I felt deceived by more.

Him or West?

"Your little boyfriend almost killed me! Do you understand that?"

"And two years of stress from you and your nameless tramp, almost killed me! So, what's your point?"

"The point is that you shouldn't have been sleeping around in the first place!"

"Really? You think that you, of all people, have the right to say that to me? Are you serious, right now?"

"Was the baby even mine? The baby that you lost? Was it mine or his?"

"If you don't know…then neither do I!"

West punched the wall with his good hand and wobbled down the hallway.

I just stood there. In silence. Wishing that I could just pack a bag and run away.

~***~

"Lava?"

It was Jerell, Tokyo's ex-husband.

"Are you okay?"

I moved away from his touch.

I was at the park with the kids.

As they played, I sat, thinking, and hurriedly wiping away my tears.

My life was so messed up.

After finding out about Kemp and what he'd done and having to see the look in West's eyes every day, and enduring his rude remarks, and comments, I just wanted to disappear.

I hated the shit-show that had become of my life, and I just wanted it to end.

I noticed the woman beside of Jerell, with a little boy. She looked at me, suspiciously, and then she moved closer to him as though I was her competition.

"I see you didn't waste any time moving on after Tokyo, huh? Sweetie, you picked a real keeper. Well, more like a real cheater. He's going to cheat on you, just like he cheated on his wife! Hell, did he cheat on her with you? Were you his side chick? Is that how you got her spot?"

She didn't respond.

"You know what, I'm sick and tired of men doing whatever the hell they want to do! But when we do it, it's a problem!"

I went off on him. I ranted on and on, and he just stood there until I was finished. The woman and the little boy walked away.

"Not that I owe you a damn thing, I barely even know you, but to set the record straight, Tokyo wanted the divorce. Not me. Yeah. I cheated. But I was trying to work it out with her. She didn't want me. I don't know what she told you, but she didn't leave me because I was cheating, again, or because I didn't want to be with her. She left me because she was cheating on me."

He shook his head and walked away to be with the woman.

Surprised by his comments, immediately, I called Tokyo.

She picked up the phone, crying.

"What's wrong?"

She continued to cry.

"Tokyo. Talk to me."

She started to mumble. "Edgar...he...he..."

Edgar.

She'd tried to play it off, but she'd probably been seeing him a lot longer than she'd let on. He was always all over her, and she would pretend not to notice. But I had. And obviously, according to her ex-husband, so had she.

"What did he do? Where are you Tokyo?"

"I just don't understand. I thought that everything was going good..."

She continued to sob, and I tried to console her.

"Can you meet me at my house? I'm right down the street. I can be home in five minutes."

She stopped crying long enough to agree.

I gathered up the kids and rushed home.

West was sitting on the couch when we walked in. He acknowledged everyone, except for me.

Moments later, I heard the knock at the front door and screamed for her to turn the knob and come in.

"I'll be right there!" I screamed from the bedroom as I changed my clothes. "Okay, Tokyo, now tell me what that fool Edgar did."

I walked into the living room to see Tokyo and West staring at each other. For a while, it was as though neither of them noticed me standing there.

"Uh, hello? What the hell is going on in here?"

Tokyo looked at me with a smirk and pulled out her phone. She tapped it and immediately, West's phone, that was on the table, started to ring.

I glanced at it.

George.

His phone said George.

She turned her phone towards me.

Her phone said West.

What the...

"Why are you calling my husband? And why do you have her number in your phone as George? Wait, so all of those times that I thought it was George calling, it was her?"

West was frozen.

And then it hit me.

"You have got to be kidding me! You. All of this time, you were the bitch that was sleeping with my husband?"

Tokyo grinned evilly.

"Well, if it makes you feel any better, he *was* my husband…first."

What?

"What the fuck is she talking about West?"

"Tell her baby," she said to him.

I lunged at her, but West grabbed my arm.

"Get the fuck off of me!"

He ignored me. And moved me to his side, while keeping his eye on Tokyo the whole time.

"West and I got married, what 19 years ago? It was a sort of rash decision. Quick, at the courthouse in North Carolina. No family or friends. I was only eighteen. If it makes you feel any better, his parents never liked me. God rest their souls. They used to tell West that I was trouble, but West loved me. Or I thought that he did. Not even a week after marrying me, he said that we'd made a mistake. He said that he had to get focused, follow his father's legacy, make something of himself, and that marriage and love would have to wait. So, we had the marriage annulled."

Her voice was different.

It was as though she was possessed or something.

It was as though I didn't know her at all.

"At the time, though I would've stayed with him, I agreed that it was for the best. Letting go of the marriage meant that I would still be able to take the scholarship that fall at Stanford, in California. I would explore new things, and new people, outside of here. So, I went to college. He stayed here. And accomplished his dreams. We never said that we would wait for each other or anything. And I didn't. I came back here, with Jerell, not planning to step out on my marriage or anything of that nature. But things just didn't happen that way, did they?" She asked West.

He had been married to Tokyo?

And no one thought to mention it?

Neither of them thought that was something that I needed to know?

I couldn't blame his family, because obviously, most of them or none of them even knew. And his father died, a year before we met, and his mother had Alzheimer's and died a few years after we were married. She'd never mentioned him being married either, so I couldn't be sure if she didn't know, or if she just didn't remember.

But my so-called friend, of three years, knew that she was my husband's ex-wife….and his mistress…

Oh! I was going to beat the hell out of her!

"Anyway, when I started working with you, I had no idea who you were. As you know, I was focused on trying to make my marriage work. And then you invited me over for the first time. He wasn't here, but I saw him in the pictures, with his wife, you, and five beautiful kids. I'd always wanted kids. So bad. But we'd never had them. And that's when I thought, wow, had I stayed behind, this could've been me. We could've still annulled the marriage, but I could've went to college closer to home, like you did, and we could've continued to see each other. Maybe we would've gotten married again, and all of this, would've belonged to me. Anyway, needless to say, I was depressed. But still, I had my faith. Until...I didn't."

She started to hum.

And then she started to sing a remixed nursery rhyme.

"Twinkle. Twinkle. Little star.

If I hit her with my car.

Do you think it'll leave a scar?

When it comes to love, how far is too far?"

She giggled. "That husband of mine had me thinking about doing some crazy stuff, I tell you. I remember sitting there, in my car. All I had to do was press on the gas. I could've ran over him and his mistress. I wanted to hit her, roll over her, and then reverse and run back over her again. She knew that she was married, but she didn't care. So, in my opinion, she would've deserved it. But I couldn't do it. I wasn't brave enough. I wasn't brave like you."

She looked at me. West looked at me too.

"That same night that I'd wanted to run them over, I went to a bar. Over two years ago. And that's when I ran into West."

I was furious! I shook my head as I spoke to her. "You knew everything. The whole time! You knew that his mistress wasn't Satin!"

"Of course." She shrugged. "It was me. Wait. Let me finish telling you the story. Oh, so yes, that night, we started to chat, and reminisce. Nothing happened the first night. But we found ourselves meeting at that bar a few times a week and somehow, things went to the next level. After a while, we fell in love. Again. The love that we'd had for each other, had was always there. It had never truly gone away. We'd never had the proper closure. Our story had never been finished. So, we started to rewrite it. We grew closer and closer. I no longer cared about what Jerell was doing. And from everything that you told me, West had stopped caring about you too."

The kids ran into the room. They called her auntie. I scowled them and sent them away. She chuckled.

"We said that it was time to leave. I told Jerell I wanted the divorce. West told me that he'd been trying to leave you, but that you were holding something over his head. He didn't know that you and Thea told me about what the three of you had done, to get him his position. I knew that the fire had to be what you were holding against him. Darling, you told me everything."

She started to hum again, and then she stopped abruptly.

"Do you know how hard it was to pretend? To not tell you that it was me? To listen to you talk about Satin, knowing that you were looking in the wrong direction? It was a workout! Some days, I just wanted to confess, but it was funny watching you go crazy, knowing that it was all for nothing. Knowing that you didn't know what the hell you were talking about."

Tokyo walked towards the pictures on the wall. She traced the frame of our wedding photo with her finger.

"Even that night of your birthday party, I wasn't arguing with Jerell. I just didn't want to be there. I didn't want to see him there with you. Leaving was the only way that I was going to be able to keep my cool. The only way that I would be able to keep our secret."

I remembered her leaving that night. She'd been arguing on the phone. Well, I thought she was. It had all been an excuse for her to leave.

"West was working on leaving you. He was going to leave you and be with me. Most nights, he didn't want to leave, so he'd started to stay. Your divorce was right around the corner; you just didn't know it yet. And then your little boyfriend had to go and bomb the courthouse and mess everything up. I was feeding West information about you and Kemp. He knew from the very moment that you told me that you were sleeping with someone else. It made us closer. It made what we were doing easier."

He knew?

West knew about my affair with Kemp, the whole time?

I moved away from him.

"But when he got hurt, he changed. On me. All of a sudden, he didn't want us anymore. He wanted you. After I'd left my husband for him. After I'd followed the plan. He almost died and all of a sudden, his plans didn't include me or us anymore. They only included you."

West didn't deny or argue with one thing that she said. He just stood there in the middle, as though he was protecting me. Or maybe he was protecting her.

"I'm tired of the men that I love playing with my emotions! Every day, I was calling him, over and over, trying to remind him of what we had, of what he promised me, of what I'd done for us, but he wanted to be stubborn. All he could do was apologize. Sorry? He was sorry that I left my husband. He was sorry that he changed his mind. No. Sorry wasn't good enough. I want what I want. I want what he promised me. I want him." Tokyo mugged West. "So, I told him, that life was about to get very uncomfortable for him. And for you. Unless you give him back."

"Tokyo," West finally spoke to her.

"Yes baby."

"Stop this and leave."

"I'm not leaving without you."

"Bitch you're not going anywhere with my husband!"

"Wanna bet? You see I've already started dabbling a little. Just to see how messy things could get. You know, that I know, how much you love Thea. And I also know that Thea killed her step-father. You know, it's our little girls secret. Well, it was. I kind of tipped off the police."

My mouth dropped open.

"You bitch!"

She hissed. "Oh, and yes, I pretended to be Satin, a long time ago, and I was the one who called Harris and told him that you were following "me". Her. You know what I mean. I told him that you were stalking *me*. And then once I came to work, Harris asked me if I knew anything about it and I told him that I saw her résumé in your car."

I couldn't believe my ears.

"I saw your little boyfriend on T.V. as a suspect, so I called in and told them to question you and that you could have been his accomplice. I told them that you were sleeping with him, and that I'd thought I heard you mention something about a bomb."

Tokyo didn't show a bit of remorse.

The sweet, faith-filled, caring lady, that I thought she was, was nowhere in sight.

"I have the knowledge of what all three of you did with the fire at the Mayor's house. And yes, I've been recording our phone conversations every now and then. You won't believe some of the stuff that I have recorded. More than enough to send you to jail, for a very, very, long time. And let's not forget the big kahuna. The fact that you killed Satin Gamal."

Immediately, my entire body tensed.

"You what?" West's voice was deep. Intense.

"She killed her. Because she thought that she was sleeping with you. She thought that she was your mistress, and that the baby that she was carrying was yours. Imagine how George is going to feel if, or when, I tell him that you killed his pregnant mistress. He doesn't have any kids, right? And from what West told me, he wants them pretty badly. He almost had one. And now, he doesn't. Thanks to you."

My mouth was so dry that when I tried to open it to speak, I couldn't.

"What is she talking about Lava? What did you do? You'd better start talking. Now!" West screamed at me.

"Oh, I'll tell you. She found out from sleeping with Kemp, Satin's brother, if you haven't caught on to that by now, that Satin had a terrible allergy to peanuts. A deadly one. Once Lava lost the baby, she couldn't stand the thought of her having a baby by you, at least that's what she thought, so, she planned to give her an allergic reaction, put her in the hospital, hoping that she lost the baby. Only, it killed her. She murdered the wrong woman."

For the first time, West moved from in between us and he sat down on the couch. He started to rub his leg.

"See, this is who you chose over me. A murderer. I mean, I'm a little crazy. But I wouldn't kill anyone. You've been trying to ignore me and push me away for weeks. You told me that you loved me, and I know that you still do. We had something that was perfect. Something that was real. You were just shaken up, by your near-death experience, but you love me. I left my husband for you, and you are going to leave her for me. Just like we discussed. Just like you promised."

West didn't comment.

I was still trying to process everything that she'd said. But all I could see was red.

"Well, I think I've done enough damage for today, don't you think? And now, that it's all out in the open, West, come on baby, let's go."

At her comments, I found the strength from up above to open my mouth and curse her. "Bitch, like I said…"

"No. Like I said…either you're going to give him back, or you're going to lose everything. Your life. Your freedom. Your kids. Your family. I'll turn in everything that I have, about what you did to Satin and I'll take down West with you. You and Thea will go to jail for setting the fire, and he will go to jail for knowing about it, I'm sure. He'll lose his reputation and his job. And you'll also go down for murder. So, the way that I see it, is that this is a win-lose situation. I win. You lose."

I started to shake my head.

Tokyo had everything. She knew everything. All of the cards were in her hand, and something told me that she wasn't afraid to play them, being that she'd already played a few.

West stood up. He looked at me as though all of this was my fault.

My entire body was shaking with rage.

"You killed Satin? Lava, what have you done?"

He started towards Tokyo, but she stopped him. "I want you to give him to me. I want you to tell me that he's mine. I want you to take off your wedding ring and give that to me too," she said to me.

I looked at her.

She held out her hand. "The police are only one call away. And since you are a killer and all, don't even think about doing something slick, like trying to kill me too, because I have stuff in place for that. If something happens to me, you're still going to go down."

She held out her hand and waited for me to reach her my wedding ring.

"Come on, I don't have all day. But the police station is open, 24-7," Tokyo threatened.

I wanted to hurt her so bad, that I started to cry. Slowly, I took off the ring that had been West's grandmother's, and I reached it to her. She twisted it on her finger.

"It looks much better on my finger anyway," she said. "Tell him goodbye." She waited on me to open my mouth.

"We have kids together."

"I'll let him see the kids. We will be one, big, happy family. He may be upset now, but he loves me. He wants to be with me. He was just confused. He'll get over this." She looked at West. "I'm doing this because I love you." He didn't reply, so she looked at me. "Tell him goodbye."

West looked at me. He stared deep into my eyes.

I was so angry. I just wanted to scream, but I didn't want to scare the kids. I felt like I was having a nightmare, and I was just waiting to wake up. I was waiting for this to be a dream. I was waiting for this to be a joke.

Not knowing what else to do, I opened my mouth.

"Goodbye."

West didn't say the words back. Instead, he wobbled towards his keys and his phone and placed them in his pocket.

"Come on baby. Finally, you get to come home."

Tokyo smirked at me and I felt as though I was going to vomit once West grabbed her hand.

He looked at me, directly in my eyes again.

Wait?

What was that?

I watched his eyes closely as he glanced at the vase, on the coffee table, over and over again.

And then he turned around, and they headed for the door.

"For what it's worth, you were a good friend," Tokyo taunted, without looking back, unknowing that I'd picked up the vase and was inching towards her.

"Oh, and by the way…"

She turned around, just in time to see me lifting the vase high in the air.

Crack!

Tokyo hit the ground and pieces of the vase fell to the ground beside her. Immediately, West knelt down to check her pulse, and I stopped the kids from running towards the living room to inspect the sound.

I got them settled inside of their rooms, and after telling them not to come out, until I came to get them, I rushed back to West.

"She's alive."

He was attempting to pace, but it was more like skipping with his injured leg.

I couldn't seem to catch my breath and once West noticed, he came closer to me, and attempted to help me breath.

"I'm sorry Lava. I really am. I wanted to tell you, but I didn't know how. It just happened."

Inhaling and exhaling, I didn't say a word.

"She knows everything. She knows too much. And, with me knowing her, I believe her. I believe that she will turn us in. These last few weeks, since I've been trying to break things off, she's been pure hell. She's been calling and texting me, like a crazy person, threatening to tell you, about us. I was entertaining her. Trying to keep her calm, but I guess she'd had enough."

"I hate you West. I hate you for putting us in this situation," I breathed.

"I know."

"I can't go to jail. I can't go to prison."

"You killed Satin?" West asked again for reassurance.

"I didn't kill her…per say. Technically, the peanut oil did. I didn't mean to. I was only trying to make her lose the baby, because I thought that it was yours!" I snatched my arm from him. "All of this is your fault! All of this is because of you!" I blamed him.

"I didn't tell you to kill nobody, and honestly, I can't believe that you would go that far!"

"It was an accident!"

West stared at me as though he didn't know me. "With what she knows about you, the only option is to give her what she wants. Unless you have a better idea."

I shook my head no.

"Then her way, it is then. It's the only choice that we have for now. I could've handled her and even the consequences of her trying to come at us about the fire. That would've been one thing. But you, going down for murder? That's something else. There's nothing that I can do about that."

"There has to be something that we can do."

Tokyo's phone startled both of us, as it started to ring.

It stopped and then it started to ring again.

We didn't answer it.

And then, my phone started to ring immediately afterwards. I didn't recognize the number, and after they called four times back to back, finally, I answered it.

"Hello?"

"Tokyo asked me to call you if she didn't answer the phone after calling her two times in a row."

It was Edgar.

From work.

"Edgar, how did you get my number?"

"Tokyo gave it to me. You know, she and I have had this thing these last few weeks."

She was bringing him into this for a reason.

"She told me if she didn't answer after calling twice, to call you and ask to speak to her. And if you wouldn't let me, to call the police. What's going on Lava?"

She was smart.

"Hell, I don't know. I haven't talked to her all day. Try her cell phone again. Maybe she's just out of reach."

Edgar didn't seem too worried about my response, so he agreed to try calling her again.

Once we hung up, immediately, he called her phone.

"She told him to call the police if she didn't answer. It seems as though she thought everything through. And she's recorded phone conversations. I don't know what you said on them, but I'm pretty sure that it's nothing good."

West stood over me. He was quiet, and then after taking a deep breath, he spoke again.

"For now, this is what we have to do. I have to go with her."

"So, I'm just supposed to be okay, with knowing that you are there…with her?"

"You don't have a choice."

"And what if there's nothing that we can do? What if there's no way out of this?" I asked him.

He took a second before answering my question.

"How would you feel about killing again? This time on purpose," West said, as he grabbed his keys, picked up Tokyo, and carried her out of the door in his arms.

~***~

"Mommy, where's daddy?" Levi asked.

He'd been asking every day, for the past three days.

I hadn't talked to West and he wasn't answering any of my calls. I'd even called Tokyo and had gone by her house, only to find that she'd moved almost a year ago. She'd lied about keeping her house. I guess that's why she'd always offered to come over to my house. It wasn't because of Jerell, like she'd said. It was because she'd known that this day would come, and she didn't want me to know where she lived.

"He had to go out of town for work. He'll be back soon."

"I thought that he couldn't work because of the fire."

"He can't. He isn't working. It's just a big, long meeting."

Levi finally seemed convinced and then he ran off to play. I was barely keeping it together.

Tokyo had been planning this right under my nose. Getting information, to use for herself. To use against me. To take my husband.

And I had absolutely nothing to use against her.

"Thea would know what to do," I mumbled and tried calling her again. Still, she didn't answer.

I couldn't wait to tell her about Tokyo, and I knew that she would have a plan.

Interrupting my thoughts, I heard the sound of keys jingling, and then the front door opened seconds later.

West.

He could barely look at me, as I rushed towards him.

Immediately, I spotted the papers in his hand.

"Three days? I've been calling! The kids have been asking about you."

"I know. I've been arguing with her non-stop for three fucking days, but she won't budge. Even when I pretended to go along with it all, she wanted more. She's a psycho. I can't believe that I didn't see it before."

He sat the papers that we he was holding on the coffee table.

"She has conversations recorded. She wasn't bluffing. I heard everything that you said about what you'd done to Satin. She played it for me. I didn't hear the ones about the Mayor's house fire, but I'm pretty sure that she has those, for real, too. She's on this whole if she can't have me, neither can you, type of thing, so there's no doubt in my mind that she won't use the recordings against you; especially the one where you're confessing to causing Satin's death."

"What did I ever do to her?" I groaned.

He sighed. "You married me."

I rolled my eyes. Obviously, that was the biggest mistake of my life!

"So, what now? We divorce? You marry her? And we all stay out of trouble?"

"That's what she wants. But that ain't happening. I filed the divorce papers to buy us some time, but don't sign them. Unless you want to. And then all of this will be over. Is that what you want?"

To be honest, I didn't know.

I just wanted to be free.

Free from a prison cell and free from West and the problems of his mistress!

A car horn wailed.

"She wanted me to come and get the kids."

"Over my dead body!"

Surprisingly, West laughed.

"I never intended on taking them. I just missed you. And them. And being here. I'm working on trying to find a way out of this. Give me some time. I swear, I'm going to spend the rest of my life making this up to you."

West walked out of the room, to go see the kids, just as Tokyo pressed down on the horn again.

I walked out of the front door, and right up to West's SUV. She rolled down the window, with a smile.

"Get the fuck out of my yard!"

She chuckled. "I will. As soon as *my man* and my soon-to-be step kids come out here. I can't wait to have them calling me Mama."

See…you know what…

Before I could stop myself, I had slapped her so hard, that her wig fell off.

"Oh. So, you want to add assault to the list of things that you should be worried about?"

That was all I was able to hear, outside of the curse words and threats that I was throwing in her direction.

Tokyo opened the car door, as though she wanted to rumble, but out of nowhere, West appeared, screaming at both of us, stating that we were making a scene and that the kids were watching.

"Get your ass in the car and let's go," he said to Tokyo.

Angry that she wasn't going to get her *lick* back, she huffed and then she shrugged and responded to West. "Okay, *Daddy*," she teased.

"See!" I reached for her crooked wig, that she'd just placed back on, and I threw it on the ground and stomped on it. She didn't bother to pick it up. She simply got into the jeep, locked her door and rolled up her window.

"Go in the house Lava."

West's eyes begged me, but I was heated!

"Get in the car with your bitch and go! This is your fault! Had you kept your dick in your pants, none of this would be happening! Just go! Go!"

I threw up my hands.

West called after me, but I stormed away. Lala was constantly calling my name and to shut her up, I picked her up, ushered the rest of the kids inside of the house and slammed the door behind me.

I tried to hold it in. I tried to be strong. But the sight of the divorce papers on the table, brought me to my knees.

My legs gave out as I allowed myself, to drop down to the floor, bawling, with Lala still in my arms.

Half of the kids started crying too, and the ones that weren't, tried to console me.

"It's okay Mommy, don't cry. Daddy says that he has a plan."

He what?

Through the tears, I looked at Lonnie.

A plan? What plan?

The last plan that I was a part of, hadn't worked out so well, and I had a feeling that his plan wouldn't either.

~***~

"Hey Lava, I know that you may be disappointed in me, considering that you and Cheyenne have a friendship, I get that, but I wanted to give you a call to ask you something."

It was George. West's cheating ass friend.

"I ran into your friend, Tokyo, the other day, and I was surprised to hear her say that you knew something about

Satin's death. She said that you were there that night, at the bar. I didn't know that you knew her," George said.

I growled.

Tokyo had been sending little reminders all week, in hopes of forcing me to sign the divorce papers.

She'd sent me a recording of me discussing my plans to get Satin to lose the baby. She'd also sent the one of me discussing the news of her death with them.

And now this.

"I didn't know her. I knew her brother."

"Kemp? He wasn't much of a people person. Never spoke. How did you know Kemp?"

"I was fucking him," I said bluntly.

I didn't care what anyone else thought these days. I was only giving West a dose of his own medicine, and honestly, with what I was going through, I wished that I'd done a bit more.

"Uh...um...okay. And Tokyo said to ask you about the baby. What baby?"

My patience was as thin as pulled out *edges*, and truth be told, I didn't really care about what he was asking me. I didn't care about him, or what had happened to her. I didn't care about anything.

"I saw your mistress at the doctor, once, when I was pregnant. I don't know if she was pregnant or not. Tokyo is just being messy. Hopefully, she wasn't. I'm not sure Cheyenne would've been too happy about that. Cheyenne…your wife…remember her?"

With that, I hung up in his face.

The phone immediately started vibrating in my hand.

West.

I wasn't speaking to him.

He was calling, but I wasn't answering. I didn't know what to say to him. Our family was ruined. Whether all of this went away or not, our lives would never be the same.

My mother's van, pulled into the driveway and I screamed for the kids to come outside. She was taking them for me, for about a week, so that I could pull myself together.

"What's wrong baby?"

"Everything."

"You look…"

"Like shit," I finished her sentence.

"Well, that's one way to put it," she sighed. "Where's West?"

"With his mistress," I answered truthfully.

Mama didn't say anything else. I guess she didn't know what to say. I kissed the kids, and then I waved at them, until they were out of sight.

As soon as they were gone, I got my purse and my keys, and I headed towards Tokyo's house.

I'd asked West for her address, before I completely shut him out. He still wasn't back at work yet, but he'd told me that she'd been going in. I'd heard through the grapevine that she'd turned down my old position and had allowed Edgar to take it. I was pretty sure that was a part of her plan to keep him in her corner for whatever reason.

I arrived at Tokyo's house and only West's car was in the driveway. I'd never been there before. But it was definitely an upgrade from where she used to live.

I got out of the car and headed towards her front door. I knew that West was going to flip out about me being there, but I was there for a reason.

I knocked, hard, and after a while, West opened the front door.

He almost looked relieved to see that it was me.

"What are you doing here, Lava?"

He was sweating.

"What are you doing?"

"Looking through her things, for something. Anything. A diary or something that may have some dirt in it to use against her, but so far, there's nothing here."

"I'm here."

West looked confused.

I pushed him backwards, inside of Tokyo's house.

She wanted to play dirty?

Let's get dirty!

"Take me to her bedroom."

I was still angry at West as I followed him, but the hatred that I felt for Tokyo, was ten times more. She was forcing me to give my husband to her. But she wasn't here now. And I was.

I looked around her bedroom. I could tell that she'd been sleeping with West. It was an upgrade from how it used to be. It wasn't junky. She had silk sheets, instead of the ten-dollar sheets from a thrift store. The room had the sun blocking curtains that West always demanded to be in our bedroom.

All for West.

All for my husband.

West turned to face me.

"What are you looking for?"

I shook my head and removed my shirt. "You."

He looked at me with curiosity.

"Make love to me. Right now. Right here. On her bed. Make love to me."

I came close to him. I knew that he wouldn't deny me, but I also knew that he didn't know what I was up to or whether or not I was serious. So, I showed him.

I got completely undress and positioned myself right in the center of her bed, on her silk sheets. I opened my legs, wide, for him to get a good look at the vagina that he hadn't seen, touched, or felt in a while.

It had been months since we'd had sex on my birthday. Even after his accident, he had tons of healing to do, so, even though he'd been trying to butter me up, sex had been the last thing on our minds.

But right now, it was the only thing on mine.

I wanted to disrespect her. The same way that she'd disrespected me, my marriage and what I thought was our friendship.

Slowly, West undressed.

Naked, I watched him walk towards me. I could tell that he was nervous about how his leg and right side of his body would hold up, confirming that he and Tokyo probably hadn't been having sex either.

"Make me feel good," I whispered, as I started to nibble on his ear. Without hesitation, West entered me and pushed deep inside of me, until I started to moan.

For the next twenty minutes, West and I made love.

If that's what you wanted to call it.

Love had nothing to do with it. Doing something because I knew that I could...did. And it didn't hurt to relieve a little sexual frustration in the process.

After all, he was still mine.

Not hers!

We finished and dressed quietly, slowly.

"Lava." West started, but I got up from the bed, and walked out of the room.

"Lava, I'm talking to you," West followed me towards the door.

"I didn't come here to talk, okay? Besides, what else is there to say?"

I opened the door, with West blabbing behind me. Just as my feet hit the grass, Tokyo's car pulled into the driveway.

She barely put the car into park, before jumping out of it. West was still talking to me, as she approached, but I had no idea what he'd said. I was looking at her.

I could tell that she was upset.

She was light-skinned, so traces of "rage red" were visible in her skin.

"What the hell are you doing at my house?"

I went back and forth, in my mind, with what I wanted to say. She still had all of the cards. I knew that I should tread lightly. I knew that she could easily ruin my life and make my life a living hell, even more than it already was.

But for the life of me, I had to do something. I had to say something. I had to have a win.

"Why are you here!" She screamed again.

"Well, you told me that I had to give my husband to you. But you didn't say that my husband couldn't still *give it* to me. If you're taking my spot, I guess now, someone has to fill your shoes, and take yours. Nice sheets, by the way," I smiled at her, and I walked away, knowing that I'd probably just sealed the deal on my fate.

And as I drove away, as I looked at her face, I knew that I'd just made, one hell of a mistake.

****

Chapter Seven

It had been wife versus mistress for the past two weeks. And unfortunately, Tokyo was winning.

She'd called the department of social services, saying that the kids were in a domestic violence household. She told them that I'd attacked her right in front of them. She also told them about the incident where I'd bust the windows out of West's jeep, and had them ask the neighbors, to collaborate her story. She even told them that I'd gotten fired from work, for stalking a potential employee, furthermore, making me look as though I was a threat and unstable.

The kids, for now *had* to stay at my parents, until further review. Just like that, she'd managed to get my kids taken away from me. And she didn't stop there.

She'd approached West's friend, George, with more "planted" suspicions. She'd told him that I'd thought that Satin was sleeping with West and that I'd been so upset when I found out that she was pregnant. She'd told him that she thought that I had something to do with her death, and that West knew something that he wasn't telling him.

So, George approached West, about me, about the truth. Apparently, George asked West to meet him for lunch, and caused a big scene. West defended me, stating that Tokyo was just starting trouble, but he said that George vowed to get to the bottom of things. He was determined to find out the truth.

So, now he was someone else that we had to watch and worry about.

And on top of all of that, Tokyo had managed to get a meeting with the Mayor...well, past Mayor now.

She'd recorded their entire conversation, telling him that she knew who was responsible for the fire at his house that almost killed his grand-daughter. He offered her everything but eternal life, to give him a name, but she'd lied and told him that she had to make sure that she would be safe first.

Just to make me sweat.

It was all one big game of control.

It was all about what she wanted.

And she what she wanted was West.

Desperate, I'd found out where her ex-husband worked, and I popped up at his job. Maybe he would know something about her, that I didn't, that could help.

I needed something. I needed anything, to bring this Hell on Earth to an end.

Every day, I told myself to just let her have him. After all he'd done, with her, and now, with all of this.

Was our marriage even worth it?

Truthfully, I wasn't sure if it was, but I refused to live under Tokyo's thumb forever, so whether or not, I wanted to be with West, in my opinion, Tokyo would always be a problem.

"What are you doing here?" Jerell questioned, removing his hard hat.

"I know that last time that we spoke, I went off, but I need your help."

He chuckled. "My help?"

"Yes. Is there something wrong with Tokyo?"

"You tell me. What do you mean?"

"I mean, is she mentally unstable? Is that why you were cheating on her? Has she ever done anything drastic or crazy, or illegal?" I probed.

He looked surprised by my questions. "Look, I don't know what you want me to say. I mean, she was just Tokyo. She treated me good. She did everything right. I'm the one who messed up. I started cheating on her. I can't even tell you why. I just did. I didn't have a reason to. It was nothing that she'd done. Nothing that she wasn't giving me. It was just me. I ruined her. I broke her. I messed her up. And by the time that I realized it, and tried to make things right, it was too late. She just wasn't the same."

Damn it!

That doesn't help.

"The only bad thing that I can say about her, is that she stayed too long. I pushed her into another man's arms. And I have to live with that forever. So, now, she's gone. No attachments, and I'll probably never see her again."

Jerell started to walk away.

No attachments?

"Why didn't you guys ever have kids?"

"Tokyo can't have kids. Something about getting an abortion after an early first marriage. Something went wrong, and she was told that she wouldn't be able to conceive again. And she hasn't."

First marriage.

She'd been pregnant by West.

"We'd tried. Went to see a few specialists. It broke her heart to hear the same thing over and over again. Kids was something that she'd always wanted. A child would've made her complete."

Seeing that Jerell didn't have anything to help, I apologized for bothering him, and I turned to walk away.

"Tell her I said hello," he shouted behind me.

Ignoring him, I got into my car and drove away.

Maybe he didn't know it, but I was sure that it was something about Tokyo that I could use against her.

Everybody has a secret.

No matter who you are, there is always something to hide. Always something that you don't want anyone to know or find out. I just had to find out what Tokyo's was.

She knew mine.

Well, except for one.

I'll never admit it, or tell anyone, but my oldest sister's, husband, was my first.

Drea and Sean weren't married at the time, but they were in a relationship.

I was sixteen.

She was the oldest of all of the girls, second to the oldest in all, and eight years older than I was. As soon as she started to bring him, Sean, around, I would catch him looking at me. I was one of the youngest, of eight kids, and always felt as though I didn't get enough attention.

But I had his.

He would watch me, hungrily, more than he watched her. I never thought that they would get married. Drea was and still is a little uppity and he, well, he looked like she'd handpicked him off of a corner out of the hood.

She wasn't his type. A blind man could see that, but she was focused, destined to be great, and her ambition was out of his world.

Why wouldn't he make it a point to stay around?

Anyway, one day, Mama told me that she was going to be late picking me up from school, and instead of waiting there for her, I walked around the block to my sister's house.

She wasn't there, but he was.

I told him that I was going to wait for Mama to pick me up. He told me that Drea was at work, but he invited me in.

For a while, we sat in silence.

He'd tried to watch T.V., but every once in a while, he would cut his eye at me. I remembered the house phone ringing, and once he got up to answer it, I could see his hard-on. Every inch of him, was attempting to bust out of the captivity of his gym shorts. He'd tried to hide it with his shirt, but I was looking. Even though I knew that I shouldn't be, I just kept looking.

He'd told me that it was Mama on the phone, asking if I'd made it there, and that she would be there in thirty minutes.

I was a virgin, but I'd long explored the world of self-pleasure, and needless to say, I was curious. And as bad as it may sound, I came on to him.

I asked him if I could see *it*.

At first, he said no, and pretended to be uninterested. I was sure that it was because I was only sixteen, and he was in his early twenties.

But I knew that he wanted me. And as soon as I grabbed for his shorts, he didn't resist, and once he started to bite his bottom lip as I touched him, I knew that he was going to give me what I wanted.

And he did.

We had thirty minutes, and he'd spent every one of them, stroking me slowly, and showing me what it was that I was supposed to do. I experienced my first orgasm, from penetration, just as Mama pressed down on her car horn.

Beep!

A horn beeped from behind me, cutting my memories short, reminding me that the light had turned green.

I pressed on the gas and shook my head.

I'd never told a soul what I'd done.

And neither did Sean, Drea's husband.

We had sex twice after that day, and we knew that we had to stop. So, we did. And then he proposed to her, shortly after that, and they got married.

Since then, and these days, although we hardly ever saw each other, except for on holidays, we would barely speak or even make eye contact.

But if ever, we were in the same room, at the same time, alone, for some reason, we would share a smile.

That was one secret that would live inside of my heart, until the day that I died, as well as trying to keep anyone else from finding out my part in Satin's death.

And I was sure that Tokyo had to have one too.

Something no one knew.

Something bad enough, secret enough, to make us even. A secret that could ruin her life, if exposed and somehow, someway, I was going to figure out what it was.

West's car was in the driveway, when I arrived at home.

He'd decided to resign from his position.

He loved that job.

But, he said that quitting, eliminated one of Tokyo's threats, and made attempting to turn us both in for the fire, less important.

Besides, though he was recovering, he'd said that despite what the doctors said, some days, he wasn't as confident in his leg, as he should be, especially when going in and saving people from fires were of concern.

He'd said that he wouldn't be able to live with himself, if while inside of a burning house, his leg gave out on him, and it caused him not to save someone's life.

West said that it was one of the hardest decisions that he'd ever had to make, but he had to do what he thought was best.

So, he'd told me that he was going to take out some of our savings, and head down the path of entrepreneurship. His grandfather had been a mechanic and had taught West plenty of things in that field.

West had always been pretty good with fixing things, especially cars, but he rarely ever got to do it. Maybe now, he could open or start something, and he would.

Currently, I was pinching off of our savings too, but we had plenty. We'd been saving for about twelve years, every single month, so for now, at least in that department, things were okay.

Just as I pulled into the yard, West came out of the front door.

"What are you doing here?"

"I'm coming back."

I looked at him.

"No. With everything going on, and all that she's been doing, Tokyo will tell the truth about what I did. And I will go to jail West. You can't."

Strangely, he smiled.

"What? What did you do?"

He opened his mouth to tell me, but his phone started to buzz. He looked more than disappointed once he saw who it was.

He pressed the button to accept the video call.

"The funniest, well not so funny, thing just happened. You remember Edgar, right? From work?" Tokyo said to him. "Well, he was having a little car trouble, so I'd been picking him up for the last few mornings. Anyway, I was busy, so he drove my car, to grab us lunch. The thing is, he never came back. And he won't ever be coming back. Because he's dead."

I could hear her, but she couldn't see me. West had the phone close to his face. He just sat there and listened.

"The police said that he was speeding, and came around a curve, but didn't appear to hit the brakes, or they assume that the brakes could have possibly gone out. They can't be sure until they check things out, a little more. You wouldn't happen to know anything about that, would you?"

West said no.

"Humph. Edgar crashed, head on with the back end of a wide load truck, and from what I know so far, my car is totaled. Now, by no means am I happy about his death, but, I must admit that I'm thankful that it wasn't me. I get the feeling that it would've been. Lucky me, I guess."

She was pure evil.

She was being sarcastic, while another innocent person was dead.

West kept a straight face and a level head. "Your car was old. I'd been telling you to get a new one for the last two years. An unfortunate accident."

She huffed. "Yes. Quite unfortunate. Be here in ten minutes to pick me up. I have to finish talking to the police. They have a few more questions, and I'm going to try my best to answer them as accurately as possible. I'm sure that they'll want to know if I've had any brake problems lately. I hadn't, but you took it to get it washed yesterday…did you? Did you notice any problems with the brakes? I mean you told me before that your grandpa taught you a good bit about cars. You would've noticed…right?"

Clearly, she was trying to intimidate him.

It was as though she was hinting at the fact that she could mention to the police that he recently drove the car and could have possibly tampered with the brakes.

She finally hung up, and West cursed and yelled as soon as he placed the phone in his pocket.

"Fuck!"

I stared at him. He'd really tried to kill her. He was desperate. Just like I'd been when I thought that another woman was having his baby.

Desperation can make a person do some crazy things. Things that they would've never even thought about doing before.

"You messed with the brakes?"

West just shrugged.

He walked towards his jeep and got in it, without saying another word to me.

Without saying goodbye.

And in my heart, I knew, that he was going to give killing her another try.

~***~

"Oh Thea!" Instantly, I started to cry, at the sound of her voice.

I hadn't heard from her in what seemed like forever. I thought that something could be wrong, or that the police had locked them up in some foreign jail.

I missed her. I needed her.

"Bitch! Stop crying and listen," she yelled in a whisper, which I didn't think was a possible.

I sniffled.

"You will never believe what I'm looking at right now. Or should I say who."

I didn't have any idea, so I waited for her to tell me.

"Who?"

Thea breathed heavily.

"Kemp."

I hadn't thought about him in forever. I guess there wasn't much to think about, since he'd pretty much lied about everything, from the day that I'd met him.

"Oh."

"Oh, my ass! You'll never guess who he's with."

"Who?"

She laughed, loud. "Look at your phone."

I saw that I had two text messages, so I opened them.

My mouth opened wide.

What was I looking at right now?

It was Kemp…and Satin.

"Thea!"

"Girl! That bitch ain't dead!"

Satin was alive!

Oh my God, Satin was alive!

This changed everything! I wasn't a murderer. I hadn't killed an innocent woman and her baby. I no longer had to carry that guilt and shame but most of all, Tokyo could no longer hold it over my head!

"She's alive?"

I was still in shock.

"Hell, yeah, and she is big and pregnant too!"

"So, she didn't lose the baby?"

"Nope. I'm sitting right here, looking dead at her, and she looks like she's about to pop! We're at some fancy restaurant in Australia."

"Australia? I thought that he was going to Egypt."

"You thought wrong. We are in Australia honey, and they're sitting right across from us. They're talking and laughing, like they don't have a care in the world. She must've known that he was about to blow some shit up. Maybe she was a part of it all too. Maybe that's why she faked her death."

The feelings of confusion and deceit that I felt, didn't come close to the feeling of relief. All I could do was breathe. Finally, I could breathe.

"Thea, you have no idea what this means!"

Quickly, I filled her in on everything that had been going on. The truth about Tokyo. The fact that she was hanging it all over my head, in order to take West from me.

"That bitch! Who would've thought that she had it in her? I told you when you first introduced me to her that something was off about her, didn't I?"

She had.

At first, Thea thought that Tokyo was weird.

She didn't understand her, and for a long time, she didn't want to have anything to do with her. But, I kept forcing her to interact with her, and eventually, they formed some kind of bond.

"She grew on me, but I knew that it was something about her from the very beginning, but you didn't want to believe me. I wish that I could come back, and personally put my foot in her ass!"

"Take a few more pictures. Zoom in on their faces. With her alive, Tokyo can't use the recordings about her death against me anymore. But she can still turn us in for the fire that we started, to help West."

Thea groaned. "And hell, I wish that we could take that back. He didn't deserve it. He didn't appreciate it. But if she does, put it all on me. I'll confess to doing it all by myself. You can say that you lied, just to look like you did something, or to cover up the truth, or hell, just say anything, but you can say that it was all me. You can say that I acted alone. It may not help, completely, since they could say that you knew about it and didn't report it, but it should soften the blow. We're never coming back anyway. And they'll have to find me, to catch me."

"What are you talking about? You said that you would be back once Ying cleared his name."

"Yeah. Well, that was before he bought a cruise ship; correction, the whole damn cruise line! Under an alias, of course. We can live on those ships forever. No one will ever suspect to look for us there. Partying non-stop, traveling all over the world. Life on the water. Pure freedom. Ying is still going to execute his plan, just in case he changes his mind, but honestly, neither of us want to come back."

"Thea, I can't go through life without you."

"You won't have to. We'll talk all the time and once you and West get this mess figured out, I'll have Ying send his pilot to get you. You can visit me, whenever you want, just say the word. Money will not be a problem. Believe me. He stole a lot of money," Thea snickered as though she didn't care that her husband was a thief. "We can't come back anytime soon, and I can't bear the thought of losing him, especially right now…because I'm pregnant!"

I screamed with excitement.

"Oh my God! Really! I'm so happy for you!"

Thea had wanted a baby for as long as I could remember.

"You're having a baby! And yet, you're still talking about putting all of the blame on you. I would never!"

"Like I said, Lava, they won't find us. We will be just fine. Just worry about you and getting your life back on track. That's what's most important. You do what you have to do, to save yourself. Ying will take care of me. Even if he has to pay off a few people to do it. Don't worry about me. You'll be surprised what people will do, for money."

Thea talked a little more about life, herself, and our family, and then she told me that the cellular reception was often horrible, so to always leave a message, if I needed her.

"I love you girl. I'm sending you some other pictures right now. Oh, and I'll send a text you, taking the blame for the fire. Just in case you need that too."

"Wait. What do you think that I should do about Tokyo? Now that I have the proof that I'm not a murderer, I can fight back, a little more than I have been. I'm still worried about the fire recordings, but setting a fire, isn't murder. And besides, other than the recordings, there isn't any proof. If there was, they would've found it years ago."

I didn't understand why I just couldn't leave well enough alone, but I just couldn't. I wouldn't.

"I need some kind of plan. To get us *all* out of this mess." I stated, hoping that Thea caught on to the fact, that no matter what she said, I wasn't going to blame everything on her, unless I absolutely had to.

Thea was quiet, for a while, and then she started to ramble. I allowed her to have a conversation, with herself, and then finally, she said something to me.

I grinned, slyly, as she spoke slowly, giving me the instructions of her master plan. It was time for me fight fire, with fire, and to get the upper hand.

~***~

"Are you having sex with her?" I asked West.

"No."

"You don't have to lie about it."

"Like I said. No."

"Well, I need you to."

The words tasted like crap coming out of my mouth. I never, ever, thought that I would say something like that.

"What? Why?"

"Because I want you to record it. Actually, I need you to record that, and a few other things."

West immediately started to fuss, and I waited patiently for him to finish.

"Would you rather be known as a cheater, or the man who help come up with some crazy, unforgettable plan, to burn down the Mayor's house, just to get a position? Besides, it's not like you haven't had sex with her before."

"That was different. I wanted to," he admitted shamefully.

"We need it. I have a plan, but I need you to play your part. Record the sex and if you can record her saying anything else that might be useful, try to get that too. Try not to say anything incriminating. I'm up to some things, on my end, that are going to push her buttons. People say and do the craziest things in the heat of the moment. And when they're upset. And I'm counting on Tokyo to slip up. I'm trying to turn the tables on her. I need for you to find me the recordings that she has about the fire. I need to be prepared. Oh, and maybe get some kind of small camera or something and put it somewhere that she won't notice it. She doesn't need to suspect anything. At all."

This was part of Thea's idea.

She'd said that it was time to give Tokyo a dose of her own medicine. We had to beat Tokyo at her own game.

The only problem we had now, were the recordings, about the fire, since the tapes conversing about Satin's death, were no longer of importance.

Thea reminded me that though we'd discussed what we'd done around Tokyo, a few times, she was sure that Tokyo couldn't have much. Thea pointed out that we'd never really gone into a lot of detail about that night, as to what all happened at the Mayor's house.

Just a few mentions here and there.

Tokyo knew the basics, and the only reason that we ended up telling her anything at all, was because one night, at the beginning of West's affair, we all got drunk, and I started to vent. I blurted out that if he tried to leave me, I would expose what we'd done.

And the explanation came after that.

I strongly doubted that Tokyo had recorded the conversation from that night. She was far too drunk, but I was sure that she'd caught a few mentions every time after that.

Still, it couldn't have been much.

So, being that no matter what we did, Tokyo still had some kind of proof on her side, the idea was to make sure that when it all hit the fan, that Tokyo's stories and theories, were discredited as much as possible.

I needed to turn her into the angry mistress.

Get her to say and do things, that in the long run we could use to our advantage.

And in the meantime, I was working on getting all of my lies in order.

With Satin being alive, it made it easier to portray me as a liar. I could say that I'd lied about everything. That I'd never really done anything to Satin. That I'd taken the credit, for something that I didn't do. That Satin faked her death and probably never really had an allergic reaction, in the first place.

I mean, that was a possibility.

I could lie and say that Tokyo was the one who suggested the idea, and that I'd just pretended to go along with it.

I'd heard the recordings, that she had in regards to Satin.

She'd sent them to me.

On one of them, I mentioned wanting the baby to die, and that I needed a plan to make her lose it. And on the other one, I was panicking because Satin was dead.

But since she wasn't....

The police were going to lose it when they saw pictures of a dead woman and their terrorist suspect...together.

And I was sure that it was going to be one hell of a surprise to Tokyo too.

Thea had even walked right up to them and said: "Hello Kemp. Long time, no see. You know, since the bombing and all. Oh, and Satin, you look pretty good for a dead woman."

She'd recorded the shock looks on their faces and sent the video to me, immediately afterwards.

Thea was crazy, but with the footage and her mentioning the bomb was perfect!

It would make it impossible for the police to question the timeline of the video and that would take care of that problem.

And hopefully, I could lie and wiggle us, out of the recordings and the problems revolving around the fire.

And if I couldn't, at that point, if it really was enough on the recordings to make us look guilty, then and only then, would I stick to the idea of me feeding her false information, deny any real involvement, and put it all on Thea.

I would say that Thea had done everything all on her own, and that I just pretended to help.

Then, I would show them the staged text messages, where Thea confesses to burning up the house, all by herself and where she'd lied about having an affair with the Mayor.

Of course, she hadn't.

But it would be his words, against hers.

Against ours, because I would lie and say that Thea told me about their affair.

I was sure that West wasn't on the recordings, since he'd never told Tokyo what it was that I was holding over his head.

He knew how to keep his mouth shut.

Unfortunately, for us, Thea and I hadn't.

So, West, would be able to say that he didn't know anything at all.

Would it work?

We couldn't be sure.

But we had to try.

We had to try to get our lives back.

Of course, Thea and Ying would be on a boat somewhere by the time that all of this would take place, so even if they did try to find her and bring her in for questioning, hopefully, they wouldn't be able to.

Without being able to find Thea, and charge her, or verify the story, all they would have was my text messages of Thea's confession, and whatever it was that Tokyo had.

The two would be two opposite stories, and without real hardcore evidence, or the missing piece, Thea, they wouldn't be able to prove Tokyo's side of the story…or mine. All they would have is accusations, and possibilities, but no real answers.

I needed to hear what was on those tapes!

"I need you to make her feel like you're falling for her. This is going to take time. Let her back in. Pretend as though you feel that there, with her, is where you want to be. Get her to play you the recordings, if you can't find them on your own. Make her think that you still love her."

West was silent.

"Do you?"

"Do I what?"

"Do you love her?"

"Are you really asking me that?"

"But you did?"

"What do you want me to say? Yes? Is that what you want to hear me say? Yes. I did. I thought...it doesn't matter what I thought. This, her doing something like this, nah, it's no love there anymore, at all. Believe that."

He was probably telling the truth.

I wouldn't love someone that was trying to force me to be with them either. Maybe that's why he'd stopped loving me.

"And you're asking me to sleep with her?"

"To save us. To save you. After all you've done to me. After all that you've put me through. And after getting us into this mess. Still, I'm here, trying to save you."

I hadn't told him that Satin was alive.

I was saving that for the day that I ended up in jail. I knew that it was going to come, and I would be ready.

West was quiet, and so, I continued with my thoughts.

"Maybe you could try and convince her that killing me would be better than trying to send me to jail."

"I'm not doing that Lava."

"Why not? Even if she says the slightest "maybe" that might be helpful. Or if she started to mention scenarios, plots or plans, that would be perfect! If she wants to take us down, then she's going down too. Plotting to murder someone, comes with charges too, you know. Definitely try to get her to say something. I'm going to be pissing her off, left and right. You just be ready to record it all."

West looked confused.

"I don't know about all of this Lava. I barely know what you are trying to do."

Hell, I barely knew what I was doing. And with Thea being unavailable, I was trying to figure it all out on my own.

"Just try to get something that we can use."

West shrugged. "I'll try."

~***~

Tears streamed down my face as I watched my husband make love to Tokyo.

She seemed to be enjoying it.

She was moaning and digging her nails into his back. She talked dirty to him, and I could tell that he was forcing himself to talk back to her.

Most of the things that I'd planned to do, to get on Tokyo's bad side, had been put on pause.

I'd gotten sick; horribly.

So bad, that I could barely get out of bed for three whole days.

But West, obviously, was on "the job".

He'd been giving her everything that she wanted from him. Telling her everything that she wanted to hear. Talking bad about me. Spending time with her and talking about their future.

All while reporting it all to me.

Once, he'd tried to get her to agree to killing me.

But he'd said that either Tokyo hadn't caught on to it, or she just hadn't taken the bait.

And then finally, yesterday, he told me that he was going to have sex with her, and that he had everything ready to record it.

When he came over this morning, with the recording, I thought that I would be okay. I knew that I needed it, to piss off Tokyo. Initially, I'd planned to upload it and share it online, but that morning, I'd thought of something better to do with it.

Either way, watching West on top of her, was the hardest thing that I'd ever had to do.

Our entire lives, our entire marriage, every important scene or memory, flashed before my eyes, and then it was as though one, by one, they shattered inside of my head like broken glass.

"Turn it off."

I popped West's hand once he tried to.

"No."

I wiped my face, and I took out my phone and snapped a close-up photo of the video, with West's *meat stick* inside of Tokyo's mouth.

Her face was clear, easy to recognize.

I made sure that you couldn't see his.

Yes! This was perfect.

"Now, you can turn it off."

West turned off the T.V. and he looked at me, with sorrow.

"We won't get past this. Will we?"

I stood up. I glanced at my face in the mirror. My eyes were blood shot red.

"I don't know. I doubt it. But whatever happens with us should be our choice. Not hers."

I sent the photo from my phone, to the printer, after using an app to type the words: "Tokyo: The Mistress. Call Me for a good time." across it. And then I added her phone number to it.

West and I just stood there, staring at each other. Listening to the annoying humming sound of the printer, as it printed copy, after copy, of the photo.

"What are you going to do with these?"

"What are we going to do with these, you mean."

I gave him half of the stack and grabbed my purse and keys and walked out the door.

West looked confused, as I got into the car.

"You go that way, I'll go this way. Let the pages fly out of the car. Put a few on cars at the grocery store, in random business parking lots, everywhere. I'm going to take a few to her job."

I couldn't imagine the look on her face once I handed a few of them out to the employees to take into the work building.

"Come on. It's lunch time. I want to catch a few of them before they go in."

"What's the purpose of this Lava?"

"To piss her off. Hopefully cause her to retaliate."

"And then what?"

"Don't worry about it. Just trust me."

"What are you talking about Lava?"

"Make sure that you are recording her and everything that she says. Press that record call button, from that app on your phone, when she calls you. Pretend that you don't know anything about this. Tell her that I must've put a camera somewhere in her room, that day that she caught me at her house. Pretend to be on her side. Just for a few more days. This is going to work. Trust me."

If this didn't make her show her high-yellow ass, then nothing would.

I drove off, and I stopped at the stop sign, just long enough to see West get into his jeep and drive the other way.

I turned down a back street and put a few of the papers in my hand. I let them fly out of the car window freely. I drove for about five minutes, putting flyers out of the window, every few seconds.

Finally, I pulled up at my old work building.

We shared the building with tons of other companies.

It was perfect.

"Lava? How have you been? I heard what happened," Doreen, an old co-worker of mine, stopped me just as I approached the building.

"I'm doing better than ever. Other than Tokyo sleeping with my husband, life is great," I revealed to her, as I reached her one of the sheets of paper.

She gasped.

I didn't care that I'd told that it was West's dick, in Tokyo's mouth, in the photo. He deserved a little embarrassment and shame.

Doreen walked away, still staring at the paper, as I started to pass them out to other people that were walking by. I laughed as I threw some of the sheets up in the air.

Folks all around me were snickering and babbling. I even saw some of the men start to dial the number.

One even asked her if he could be next, once she'd answered.

Hurriedly, I walked away.

I got into my car and laughed so hard, that I cried.

That will teach her not to put stuff in her mouth, that didn't belong to her.

And then, like clockwork, my phone started to ring.

Tokyo.

Doreen must have shown her the print out and told her that she'd gotten it from me.

The first time, I let her go to the voicemail, and when she called right back, I knew right then and there that she was probably as hot as the Devil's piss.

I saw her walk out of the building, and all of the men, started to approach her, so she ran back inside.

I answered the phone, and immediately, hit the record button on the app to record the call.

"Hello?"

"I swear to God…I'm going to kill you! Bitch, you are done! Do you hear me? Done! You think I've ruined your life so far, I promise you, you ain't seen anything yet! Let's see how you like what I do to you next!"

Ooh…was that a threat?

To kill me?

Had she admitted to trying to ruin my life on purpose?

I laughed in her ear as I pressed stop on the recording and hung up on her, while she was still yelling.

I replayed the recording and I listened to her threaten my life, and to her admit that she had an agenda.

I placed the phone in the cup holder, and I smiled as I headed towards the courthouse.

Gotcha'!

****

Chapter Eight

"Twinkle. Twinkle. Little star.

If I hit you, with my car.

I'm praying that it leaves a scar.

For your sake, don't make me go that far."

I taunted Tokyo with my own version of her scary nursery rhyme.

She and West were both dressed up.

He'd known that I was on my way, but she'd had no idea what was about to happen.

I got out of my car and skipped towards them.

West pretended not to know anything about the papers. He'd sworn that he didn't know how I would have gotten the footage, and he'd helped her tear her bedroom a part. West allowed her to find the *not-so-hidden* camera.

She'd never noticed the small nanny camera that sat upright in a candle holder, right across from the bed.

West convinced her that it was probably recording them, at that very moment, though it wasn't, and he'd said that Tokyo stomped on it, without hesitation.

West blamed it all on me.

He convinced her that I'd hidden the camera, that day that I'd come over, and told her that was probably my purpose for showing up at her house in the first place, and that I'd probably been watching them the whole time.

He'd said Tokyo had questioned, how I knew where she lived, and he'd told her at some time or another, I must have followed one of them.

That day, West secretly recorded Tokyo saying all kinds of things.

She was mad as hell; especially because she'd been receiving never-ending phone calls, from strangers, looking for a good time.

She'd said that there was no way that she could ever show her face at work again, thanks to me, and that I had to pay for what I'd done to her.

I'd been waiting for something to happen.

But it never did.

So, I'd decided to jump ahead of it all.

It was time to get it all over and done with; especially since I'd missed my period, and I had a feeling that I was going to be pregnant again.

I'd put some things in place.

I'd prepared my lies.

And now, it was time to stop playing her games, and see what it was that she really had on me.

It was time for her to give my husband back to me.

"You're really about to piss me off," Tokyo said.

"It's better to be pissed off, then to be pissed on. Tell me something, what are you getting out of trying to force him to be with you? What's the point? He's only here because of what you know...well, because of what you think you know," I said to her.

"I'm not forcing him to do anything...not anymore. I just had to remind him of what we had. He remembers now. Tell her West."

She nudged him, but he moved away from her.

West walked towards me.

"Oh. I see. So, both of you think that this is some kind of game, huh?" She asked.

"No. But you do. And I'm done playing with you. To be honest, after all of this, I'm not even sure if I want him. Lord knows, he doesn't deserve me. And if we both come out of this, on top, I'd probably never look at him the same. I'm sure that every time I look at him, all I'll see is the hate that I have for you. But I'll tell you one thing, you will never have him. He, this man right here, he belongs to me,"

I looked at West. "And he isn't going anywhere, with anybody, unless I want him to."

"Wrong. He's about to go with me right now. We have reservations."

I laughed at her.

"Wrong! No, you don't. West gave me the information earlier. I already canceled them."

Tokyo looked at West as he stood right in front of me. I grabbed the back of his head, and I kissed him.

And as I stepped out of my shoes, I knew that all hell was about to break loose.

This was it.

I already knew that I was going to jail that day.

But not before I beat the hell out of Tokyo.

"I'll see you at the jail," I whispered to West.

He nodded his head.

Once my bare feet touched the ground, I pulled away from him, and immediately, and without her expecting it, I went for Tokyo's head.

I'd already instructed West not to stop me and not to break us up. She deserved this good ole' ass whoopin', that she was about to get.

I wasn't sure if I was pregnant or not, so just in case, I didn't fight fair. I kicked and punched Tokyo. I bit her and pulled her hair. I clawed at her eyes, all in attempt to make sure that she didn't get the best of me.

I'll admit, she wasn't as easy to overpower, as I'd hoped she would be.

She fought back and stood her ground, but once she fell, I beat her like she stole something; which for two whole years, she had.

Finally, the police arrived, and pulled us a part.

A nosey neighbor had called them, and the female officer seemed to be disappointed in West, for doing nothing at all to stop us.

Tokyo screamed at me as the male officer threw me into the back of the police car.

West stood there, looking at me, the whole time, as the officer started talking to him.

With the windows down, I could hear Tokyo calling me a murderer and telling them that she had proof that I'd been the cause of someone's death.

She looked like a crazy person, with one shoe on, and one shoe off, and her shirt was ripped, exposing her chest.

The female officer, walked to her car, and I saw Tokyo get on her cell phone. A few minutes later, the female officer, approached Tokyo, and started to put her in handcuffs.

I smirked.

I'd taken out a warrant on Tokyo for communicating threats. I'd taken the recordings to the police station and pretended to be scared for my life. I fake cried and everything. I told them that she was my husband's crazy and jealous mistress, and that she'd been threating to kill me.

Showtime.

"Mrs. Mason, Ms. Hall is pressing assault charges against you."

"And I'll be pressing them right back. She hit me first. Ask my husband. He's my witness," I lied.

"She says that you attacked her."

"She's lying. She's crazy. Check the warrant against her. She threatened to kill me."

The detective sat down in front of me.

"Funny, you mentioned kill. She claims that you are responsible for the death of Satin Gamal. She says that you knew that she was allergic to peanuts, and that you put peanut oil into her drink. She says that she can prove it."

"She's lying."

"Why would she be lying about something like this?"

"Because, she's crazy. Do you have my phone? Get it. I have something to show you."

Detective Williams left out of the room.

After a few minutes, he came back with my phone.

"Passcode 1316. Go to the photos and videos."

He did as he was told, and I told him what to look for.

"You mean that Satin Gamal?"

I said once the video started to play.

"She's not dead. Apparently, they faked her death. I guess when your family has tons of businesses and money, you can do that. I'm not sure how, or why, but Satin Gamal is alive and well. Looks like you have a few doctors or something that to question. Not me. Obviously, they had some help pulling this off. And as you can see, she's sitting with your bombing suspect. Her brother...Kemp Gamal."

The detective watched the video again and listened to Thea's words.

"How did you get this? And who is this? Speaking?"

"My cousin Thea."

He looked at the papers.

"Thea? Yes. Here's what she said about Thea. She says that Thea killed her step-father and that you, Thea, and your husband were the ones who set the Mayor's house on fire, a few years ago, causing the fire that almost killed his granddaughter."

"What? She's crazy! Me and my husband would never do anything like that!"

"And Thea?"

"I mean she's a little crazy, but that's something you would have to ask her."

"And where is she?"

"Who knows. Traveling or something. Where's this so-called evidence of these allegations? I want to see whatever it is that this crazy lady is claiming to have. As you can see, I didn't kill Satin. You saw that with your own eyes. Tokyo is evil. She wants me out of the picture. She's a mistress, who is upset that my husband wants to come back home. Nothing more. Nothing less."

The detective gave me a look of uncertainty.

"She says that she has the proof in a safe place."

"So, you're going to hold me until she brings it?"

"Unfortunately, the only thing we could hold you on is the assault charge, but since your husband already posted your bail, I have to let you go. But I have a good feeling that I'll be seeing you again. And soon."

That's it?

He was letting me go?

I was expecting Tokyo to have the recordings on her phone or e-mail or something, ready to play them. Ready to try to put me away for a very long time. I hadn't expected to be walking right back out of the jail, to go home, so soon.

"I'll see you around," he said to me, as I made my way towards West.

West and I didn't speak until we got into the car.

"Oh my God!"

I exhaled.

I'd felt as though I was going to faint the entire time that I was inside of the jail.

West was rambling so fast that I couldn't keep up.

"What happened in there? What did they say? What did Tokyo tell them? Do they believe her?"

I told him everything that the detective said to me.

"Why didn't she present the proof?"

"I don't know. It doesn't make sense. I heard them. You heard them. She played the one where you were panicking about Satin's death…"

"Oh yeah. About that. Satin isn't dead."

"What? What do you mean?"

I showed him the pictures and the video. The detective took copies of the photos and video, but he allowed me to keep my phone.

"Thea saw them. Satin and Kemp. Together. And she took pictures and sent me this video. I told you to trust me. I already knew that Satin wasn't dead. Tokyo is going to lose it, once she takes them the recording and the detective tells her the news, about Satin."

West was quiet.

As though he was still trying to process it all. Finally, he spoke.

"So, you didn't kill her?"

"No. I didn't. Now, the only worry we have is the fire issue. That's all that we have to worry about. And they didn't have her proof, so they couldn't hold me. That's why they let me go."

"Yes. But for how long?"

"That…I don't know."

I'd long since tried to remember every time that we'd mentioned the fire in front of Tokyo. I was hoping that whatever she had, at best, would be seen as circumstantial.

West was so relieved that I wouldn't go down for Satin's death. He smiled about it. He thanked God, and for some reason, I started to smile at him.

He did care.

He cared about me.

I told West to take me to see our kids.

We talked about the situation the whole ride there and once we got there, we placed on fake smiles, but that didn't last for long.

As soon as my sisters, Janay and Declora spotted West's car, since they lived on the same street as our parents, they came running.

They both had heard bits and pieces, about what was going on between West and I, but they did know that West was at fault, and they were letting him have it!

I started trying to explain a few things to them, but Mama told me that it was none of their business, what I did with my husband.

Seeing that they weren't going to back off, we left in a hurry and told the kids that we would be bringing them home soon, not knowing if we were telling them a lie.

We didn't know what was going to happen.

We didn't know what was next.

West and I talked and talked, the whole ride towards home.

Well…

What used to be home.

We arrived, just as the orange flames pushed themselves out of the living room windows.

Hearing the sirens in the distance, West hopped out of the car, and rushed as close to the house as he could.

Our house.

Was on fire.

Our home.

Was gone.

~***~

"Did you or did you not try to kill Satin Gamal?"

"Not. Like I said, it was all a lie. To *save face*, you know, to act like I had it all under control."

"Explain," the detective said.

"Why? Why does any of this matter? She isn't dead."

"No. She isn't. But maybe I can pull an attempted murder charge out of all of this."

"Like I said. It was a lie."

"Humor me."

I huffed. "I wanted them to believe that I was handling things. I didn't know at the time that Tokyo was sleeping with my husband, too."

"Oh. So, Satin was also sleeping with your husband? As well as Ms. Hall?"

"Yes." I lied. "But as I said, I didn't know about Tokyo at the time. Anyway, I wanted to make them think that I was bold enough to do something like that. It was Tokyo's idea in the first place. You know, to take matters into my own hands, and to do something crazy."

It wasn't but, it was her word against mine.

We hadn't seen or heard from her.

We knew that she'd been the one to burn down our house, but we couldn't prove it. She'd gone quiet, and we'd thought that maybe she'd had enough, just like we had.

Maybe she would just go away.

But then, the detective showed up at Mama's, to tell me that they needed me to come back in for a few questions.

Tokyo had turned in her proof.

She'd turned in the recordings.

"I saw Satin's story on the news, and I pretended as though I did it. I wanted them to think that I did it, but I didn't."

The lies rolled off of my tongue effortlessly.

"You were at the bar that night? Right?"

"Yes. We were. But I was there because I was invited. Kemp asked me to come for his birthday. I was sleeping with him. But I'm sure that you know that already. I saw

Satin that night, but I never even spoke to her. Pull the tapes from the bar that night. You'll see. I'm sure that they have some kind of cameras or something."

The detective scratched his nose.

I already knew that he couldn't get to the tapes because Kemp had destroyed them.

"So, everything that you said was a lie?"

"Yes. Unless you can prove otherwise. Other than that, what else would you call it?"

"Maybe you were a part of helping her fake her death. Maybe you knew what was about to happen with the bombing."

I growled at him. "I would never! Had I known about the bomb, I would've said something."

"To who?"

"Somebody. Furthermore, why are we talking about this? I didn't know about the bomb and that's, that. When it all boils down to it, the lady is alive. This little murder confession, as you call it, means nothing, without someone actually being murdered. I had nothing to do with it. Nothing to do with her allergic reaction. If she even had one. What if she didn't? What if she never even had an allergic reaction that night? If they lied about her death, I'm pretty sure that they could've lied about that too. Maybe that allergic reaction was all a part of their plans to fake her death and help her disappear. So, even if you tried to get me for "attempted murder" how could you be sure that any of it ever happened at all? How can you be sure that the whole reaction wasn't staged? I'm convinced that it was. And the doctors involved, that reported her death, are liars; so, you can't ask them. I mean you can, but after lying to the world, that she was dead, who's going to believe them? I doubt a judge or jury will."

He laughed.

"You seem to have an answer for everything." The detective looked at me suspiciously, but he knew that I was right. I guess watching all of those law and criminal court shows, had actually done some good.

"And this fire? Tell me about it."

"What fire?"

"The one where you said, and I quote: *Just like that fire that we started. And for what? For him?*"

My body tensed.

I tried to think of something to say, but the detective spoke again.

"Yeah. Use that. Hang that shit over his head. If he thinks that he's leaving you for another bitch, then he will

be leaving her too, because his ass will be going to jail!
Men are so ungrateful."

He smirked. "I'm assuming that these are the words of Thea. Where is she by the way? Still in China?"

Tokyo must've told him that.

"I don't know where she is, but we were talking about something else. We weren't talking about whatever it is that Tokyo told you."

"The Mayor. Ms. Hall says that you were talking about the fire that occurred at the Mayor's house. Isn't that what you're referring to?"

I shook my head. "Nope."

I'd listened to all three of the recordings where the fire was discussed. They all pretty much said the same thing and none of them mentioned the Mayor.

Not once did we say his name, or even the word.

"I didn't hear anything about it being the Mayor's house on those recordings. Maybe that's what Tokyo assumed, but neither of us said that. And we wouldn't have because that's not the fire that we were referring to."

"Why would Ms. Hall assume that you were referring to burning down the Mayor's house?"

"I'm not sure. But assuming, will make an ass out of you and me...won't it? I don't know why she thought that, but she's wrong."

"Then why would your husband be going to jail? Why would you be hanging it over his head? To keep him from leaving you?"

"We were talking about another fire."

"What fire?"

"Not that one."

"Then which one?"

I huffed, to buy myself time as the wheels in my head started to turn. "It was from a long time ago. But it wasn't West and I. It was just Thea."

I had to do it.

I couldn't think of anything else to say and I knew that he wasn't going to let up. But I was going a different route than expected. West had the screenshots of Thea's confession in his cell phone. I'd sent them to him, the day before I fought Tokyo, and erased them from my home. I hadn't want them to see or find them. I only wanted to use them if I had to, and after the recording. But since they barely had anything, and didn't mention the Mayor, I was going to still use Thea, but I was going to say something else.

"Thea?"

"Yes. She burned down someone's house before."

"Whose?"

"I don't remember his name. Anyway, I accidentally let it slip out, in front of Tokyo. She and I were drinking, and I told some of Thea's business. So, I tried to fix it. I tried to cover it up. I tried to keep Thea's secret. So, I made up a story, just for Tokyo. But it still didn't involve the Mayor. I don't know where she got that from."

The detective laughed aloud.

"Do you lie for a living? Like professionally? My God woman!"

"I'm not lying."

"So, why were you hanging it over West's head?"

"Because, he knew about it. The real fire. I'd told him about what Thea had done, and being the Fire Chief and all, I'm pretty sure he was supposed to do something about it, but he hadn't turned her in or did anything at all. That's what I was holding over his head. The fact that he knew and did nothing."

"So, he knew that she set someone's house on fire?"

"Yep. I told him. But I didn't tell him who. So, he knew of it. And the way that he loved his job, when I started threating him, with ruining his reputation, he did whatever I wanted him to do. As the Fire Chief, knowing that someone committed the crime of arson, and not reporting it, I'm sure is a big deal."

"That it is." He stared at me. "Hmm…I'm not convinced. And you do know that knowing, is just as bad as doing it."

"Not really. Depends on how you look at it. Like I said, he didn't know all of the specifics. Neither did I."

"So, this Mayor story, is all in Ms. Hall's mind?"

"Yes. All to get me locked up, so that she can be with my husband. Those recordings don't say anything. She's grasping at straws. She has nothing. What she thought she had was a murder confession. I bet she won't see that coming. I bet she's going to pass out, when she finds out that Satin isn't dead. If you haven't told her already."

The detective stared at me.

"I'm missing something. I know it."

"I doubt it. Find Thea and ask her. I remember that fire. The one at the Mayor's house. West put his own life at risk, to go back in there and save that little girl. He could've died. Why would he do all of that if he knew about the fire? Why would he risk getting himself killed? A little extreme, don't you think?"

"Maybe he didn't. Maybe your husband didn't know. But I think that you did. And maybe your cousin. And then you told your husband afterwards. Right?"

"Wrong."

The detective stared at me for a long while, and then he walked out of the interrogation room.

Inside, I was nervous. I had knots in my stomach, the size of Texas, but I didn't show it. I played it cool.

In a way, I was upset.

Had I known that was all that Tokyo had, I wouldn't have played nice for as long as I did; after I found out that Satin was alive.

Everything that she had was circumstantial.

A possibility, and with me never saying what house, and whose house, it just made it a classic tale of he said, she said. There was no way that they could actually pin anything on me, or us, unless they went back to the Mayor's old house and somehow found new evidence.

My lawyer rushed into the room.

I scowled him for being late, and he assured me that the conversation was over.

They didn't have anything.

Nothing strong enough to hold me, yet again.

The detective came back in, and my attorney spat a few things at him, and then he told me to stand up.

"One last question, how did your wedding ring get there?"

I stared at him.

"I went by the Mayor's old burnt down house, you know, just to look around, before I brought you in. The burnt house is still just sitting there, but strangely, he keeps the grass cut. Anyway, I looked around for a while. Underneath the steps, and in all of the bushes, and what do you know, I found this."

He sat a clear bag on the table with my wedding ring inside of it.

"I noticed you don't have a ring on your finger. It's your wedding ring, isn't it?"

That bitch!

"Yes. It is, but Tokyo put it there!"

"She put your wedding ring, at the Mayor's house? Under a pile of dirt?"

"Yes. She asked me for it. On the day that she...when..."

I exhaled.

My lawyer sat down in the chair and told me to sit down beside of him.

"I gave the ring to her. On the day that West moved out and moved in with her. She must've put it there."

"Maybe you should start asking your lawyer what it is that you should say next, because…"

"I know what it looks like, but I'm telling the truth. Okay, fine, why wouldn't they have found it when they went over the scene, what, five years ago?"

"Maybe they overlooked it."

"They overlooked it? At the Mayor's house? After someone tried to burn it down? They overlooked that?"

"Maybe."

I tried to think.

"Ask my husband. He'll tell you."

"Or he'll lie. For you."

My attorney spoke to me, but I wasn't listening.

Think Lava! Think!

"Oh! We took family photos, two years ago. On the one by myself, my hand is underneath my chin. I'm wearing my wedding ring on the picture. That was two years ago. Check the dates, at the studio, where we had them taken. The fire at the Mayor's house was what, five or so, years ago? Go to my house…"

"Your house burned down, remember?"

Shit.

I stuttered for a second, but my thought came to me. "Go to my Mama's house. She has a copy of the photo. I'm wearing my wedding ring. Call "Blue Jaybirds Studio" and look at all of their proofs of the photo shoot. I'm wearing the ring. Check my social media. I'm pretty sure I have pictures where you can see my wedding ring on my finger. I'm not lying. She put it there. Tokyo put it there. She's trying to set me up. Go and get the photos."

Detective Williams looked at me. "Mrs. Mason, for your sake, you had better hope that I find something that gives me just a 1% feeling that you may be telling the truth, or you will be going down for arson. And in case you didn't know, it's a minimum of 5 to 7 years in prison, if convicted. With the discussion of the fire on the recordings, and the ring at the scene of the crime, and if we can put Tokyo on the stand, I'm sure if this goes before a judge, that you're going to have a very bad day."

He left us alone for a long while.

I had forgotten all about my ring.

It seems as though Tokyo had always been thinking one step ahead of us.

She wanted West so bad, that she was willing to do anything to keep him. She was willing to do anything to get rid of me.

I sat there for what seemed like forever, and then finally, the detective came back into the room again.

He was holding the family picture.

"Well, you're definitely wearing the ring."

I exhaled.

"I checked a few pictures on your social media too. You have a video, from a few months ago, with you, Tokyo and Thea in it. I guess before the truth came out. Anyway, on the video, you are definitely wearing this ring. The same purple diamond in the center and everything."

I exhaled.

"Maybe Tokyo did plant the ring. Maybe you are telling the truth about that. But I do believe that you are guilty. And I will prove it. Just not today."

He told me that I was free to go…again.

And I couldn't have gotten out of that jail fast enough!

I was surprised to see that West wasn't there, and when I'd called him, he said that he had stayed at Mama's, once he'd followed the detective to get the picture, and that he was on his way back.

Just as I hung up the phone, a fancy black town car, pulled up, directly in front of me.

The window rolled down.

Kemp.

He had to be a bold soul to roll up in front of the jail; right next to the courthouse that he'd bombed and burnt half of it down.

"Get in."

I shook my head. "No."

"Lava. Come on. Get in."

"Why?"

Kemp slid over towards the door.

"Because I'm trying to save your life. Now, get in."

What?

I stood there for a while and then finally, I reached for the door handle and got in. The car pulled away.

"I thought you were in Egypt."

He looked like something out of a magazine. His hair was pulled into a ball at the back of his head. He had on a collared shirt, and some slacks, with a single gold chain around his neck.

"I've been a little bit of everywhere. I'm sure Thea told you."

"She did. She also told me that Satin wasn't dead."

"She isn't."

"So…"

Kemp looked at me.

"Satin is my wife, Lava."

I looked at him in disgust for the first time.

"We had our roles to play. Being siblings was our cover-up and had been for a few years. But she is my wife."

"The same wife, who you were arranged to marry? With the rich family?"

"One in the same. And her family is rich, but they have different means of making money. Some good. Some…not so much."

His wife?

Satin was his wife?

"So, that whole story about your wife and child, being killed?"

"I'd flipped the story a little bit. Satin was driving, drunk. But she is my wife, and it was my pregnant sister who died."

Wow.

"So, it was all a lie?"

Kemp looked directly into my eyes. "Everything that I ever told you was a lie."

Well…damn.

"Pretty much, all of it. Except for how I felt with and around you. Playing our roles, got us into some sticky situation. Hell, she even got pregnant. By another man. And I. I met you. Usually, I stayed to myself. I only engaged with people when I had to, but I couldn't resist you."

"And the bombing?"

"Yes. I did it. It was what I was supposed to do. Satin had her own mission; which she also accomplished. Oh, and another thing that I didn't lie about was her allergy to peanuts. That part was true, and you putting the peanut oil into her drink, was just in time."

"Wait, I never told you that it was peanut oil."

"You didn't have to. That's what doctors are for. Anyway, that was the perfect way to make her disappear. But she did have a reaction, but one of the doctors that *we* pay, fixed her up, and then pretended as though she'd died. And just like that, Satin Gamal, was gone. She was free to go on to her next assignment and never be seen or heard of again."

"Assignment?"

"Yes."

I stared at him for a while, but I knew that I had to say something.

"So, you are a terrorist?"

"According to the news, I guess so. But you'll be surprised by who I actually work for."

"Who?"

"I'm not at liberty to say. All I know is that I didn't expect to meet you."

I didn't know what to say.

Why couldn't he just be *fine*…and normal?

I had horrible taste in men!

"I only came back to give George his son. George was Satin's assignment. She'd only fooled around with him, because he's married to Cheyenne…who is the daughter of one of the most respected State Senators. She had a purpose. She only used him to find out whatever she could about his wife's father. We needed a little dirt on Mr. State Senator. And we found some. But in the midst of it all, Satin got pregnant. But the allergic reaction didn't affect the baby at all. She carried him and had him. But we can't keep him. Besides, there isn't any room for a child, in our world. That's why in twenty years, we've never had our own. So, I took a risk, to bring the baby back here, to him. And to see you."

I couldn't believe my ears.

You would think that nothing would surprise me after what West and Tokyo had put me through, but I was appalled by his revelations.

"So, everything with her, Satin, was a lie as well?"

"Yes. Anything, everything, including our names. Including our "businesses". They do belong to our network, but nothing else is true."

"And me? How did you know that I was at the jail?"

"I know a lot of things. And as I said, we have a few people, everywhere. But I can help you. I want to. I need to." Kemp, or whatever his real name was, turned to face me. "Tell me what you need me to do."

I looked at him confused.

"What do you need me to make go away? Whatever it is, I can get it done."

The car stopped driving and I noticed that we were back in front of the jail.

"I told you a long time ago, that I wasn't a good man. That part about me was true. I've done things. Horrible things. And I'm not trying to justify them. I just learned to live with them. And I want to do something that will help you. I've never loved another woman, other than my wife, but I would be lying if I said that I didn't care about you." Kemp touched my hand. I allowed it. "We've said goodbye, over and over again, but I want my final goodbye to be something that you will remember. Something that will give you your life back. So, tell me, Lava what is it that you need?"

I could tell in his eyes that he was serious.

He'd help me from losing my mind during the infidelity, and now he was here, out of nowhere, offering to help me out of this mess.

Why my guardian angel gotta' like blowing people up and shit?

Out of the car window, I saw West running up the steps towards the doors of the jail. I wasn't sure why, but for some reason, I smiled.

I had no idea what I wanted, but I needed everything, all of the problems, including Tokyo, to go away so that I could figure it out.

"Oh, and Thea told me to tell you hello."

"What?"

"Her husband, Ying, did a little work for us. She didn't know at the very beginning, but she knew when we met them in Australia."

"Wait, so you were meeting Thea and Ying?"

"Yes. Ying paid us to work with a few people to clear his name. Ying instructed her not to tell you that she'd met with us, but when she took the video, I was sure that she wasn't going to listen."

I'm going to kill Thea for not telling me everything!

"I met them, off of the coast of Puerto Rico, before I came back here. I had to pick up his final payment, to pay off everyone involved in the case that was against him. He's in the clear now. You'll be seeing something on the news about it soon. They can come back, whenever they are ready, but I don't think it will be anytime soon. Thea thanked me for working with her husband to clear his name, and at that point, she told me everything that you were going through. And then she cursed me out and told me to help you. And to tell you that she said hello."

Thea was always looking out for me.

I was glad to hear that Ying was out of trouble. But I was disappointed that they still wouldn't be coming back home.

"All you have to do is ask, Lava," he said.

I took a while to get my thoughts together, and then finally, I nodded my head.

I took a deep breath.

"Okay. I need…"

~***~

"Has anyone contacted you? From the jail? I'm sure that someone has picked up his cases, by now," West said.

"Nope. I haven't heard a thing."

A month ago, Detective Williams was gunned down, after arriving at a scene that was supposed to be a robbery---the only thing was, was that the thieves hadn't taken or stolen anything.

It had Kemp's name all over it.

And since Detective Williams had been killed, all of the questions about the fire, the Mayor and the recordings, had abruptly, and most likely, indefinitely, stopped.

It was like, all of the allegations had just disappeared.

No one ever called.

A new detective, never showed up.

Nothing.

I watched West take a few of the boxes inside of our new rental home. He worried all the time, about what would happen, but I assured him that everything was going to be okay.

I never told him about my conversation with Kemp. It wasn't any of his business, as to what Kemp had promised to do for me.

That day, at the jail, I'd asked him to fix my life.

I told him that I just wanted a normal life back.

No mistresses.

No cops.

No jail.

No worries.

Just me and my five kids…well about to be six.

I was pregnant.

And I told Kemp that too.

Hoping that he could do it, I'd asked him to make all of the suspicions, and allegations, disappear. He'd told me that it wouldn't be a problem.

So, lastly, I told him that Tokyo had to go.

I didn't tell him to kill her; but I didn't tell him not to either.

I just told him that I never wanted to see her again.

And I hadn't.

That day, Kemp agreed to fix things for me, but he'd also made me promised him that I would give my marriage another try.

He'd said that sometimes, love just needed a little reminder. He sounded just like Mama.

Kemp said that after all of this, West would spend the rest of his life, proving himself to me, and that there was no greater love, than love…after forgiveness.

I noticed that the flag on the mail box was up, so I walked towards it, to put it down.

Out of habit, I opened the mailbox.

My wedding ring was inside.

The sticky note underneath it said:

"I hope he never gives you another reason to take this back off. Goodbye Lava…K."

Kemp.

I didn't even begin to wonder as to how he knew about the house.

Just for the hell of it, at the time, I'd agreed to do what he'd asked of me. To give my marriage another try.

And here, today, I was glad that I did.

Putting the ring back on my finger, I smiled at the kids, as they started to play in the yard.

Life had been better.

Different.

And I was sure it was because Tokyo had disappeared.

I watched the news, every day, just to see if her body popped up somewhere.

But it hadn't.

It was as though she'd just vanished.

I'd even driven by her house, a few times, just to see if her car was there, but it never was.

Being nosey, I called the job and pretended to be a client, just to see if she'd ever gone back to work, but they said that they hadn't heard from Tokyo in weeks.

I didn't know where she was.

Or where she'd gone.

Or if she was dead or alive.

But if I never saw her again, it would still be too soon.

She'd tried to take my life away from me.

She'd tried to take my husband.

She'd tried to take everything.

I greeted George as he pulled into the yard.

He and West were back on speaking terms and he apologized for his behavior, once West told him that Satin was still alive, and that she'd faked her death.

I found it strange that he didn't have the baby.

Kemp had said that he'd only put his freedom at risk, to bring the baby back, to George, but George never mentioned having the baby.

Maybe Satin had second thoughts.

Speaking of baby, Thea was starting to show. She sent me pictures all the time, but she did confirm, that they didn't plan to come back home…at least not for good. She'd said that now that it was okay to visit, they would. But she seemed happier than ever before.

And that was all that I could ever ask for.

West came out of the house, with a smile on his face, and I thought about all we'd gone through.

These last few weeks, between us, had been almost magical.

I guess we were both just so thankful for second chances. We both were excited for new beginnings.

West was jumping through hoops to please me. He was acting like his old self again. He was consistently finding ways to show me that he loved me, and it was working too.

Every day, I was falling back in love with my husband, even though I hadn't expected to.

I realized that all of the drama, in a way, had been one of the best things that had ever happened to me.

I smiled at West, knowing that all of the heartache and the pain, had given him back to me.

~***~

Tokyo

Sitting across the street from Lava and West's new House…

We sat there, watching them, and then finally, we drove away.

"Not the ending that I was hoping for, but I guess it was still a job well done," she said.

I stopped at a red light and touched the side of her face.

What I felt for her, I couldn't really explain. But it had been enough to make me do all of those crazy things.

"It's okay. They can have each other. We have one another."

She beamed.

"So, that little divorce of yours, is final, huh?"

I joked with her, already knowing the truth.

She laughed. "Silly, you don't need a divorce, from your husband…if he's dead." She laughed again. "Thanks to Kemp."

I smiled at her.

"Then how about we disappear?"

I headed towards the highway.

"I thought you'd never ask. I would like that. I would like that very much."

"Where should we go?"

"Anywhere but here," she said.

"Anywhere sounds good."

I turned up the radio, and rolled down all of the windows, as I entered the highway, heading towards forever with…

Drea.

Lava's oldest sister.

We'd met at a support group, a few years ago.

It was a group for abused women.

We weren't being physically abused; but emotionally, and mentally, we were both going through hell.

She'd hid it from her family, but her husband, Sean, was just as bad as Jerell.

All he did was cheat on and lie to her too.

We'd started to bond, and form a friendship, and then one day, she invited me out for drinks.

She told me, that Sean had been diagnosed with cancer. And at that time, they weren't giving him that long to live, so he'd made a few confessions.

One of them included sleeping with Lava, her sister.

Drea was heartbroken.

She was furious!

I'd just started working with Lava and I didn't know much about her. I didn't even know that they were sisters, at first. And in the beginning, I really didn't know that she was married to my ex-husband, West.

Drea was angry, and all she ever talked about was how happy Lava and West were, and how she didn't deserve him, after what she'd done behind her back.

After she'd had sex with her husband.

Even though he'd told her that it was years ago, still, she hated her Lava. And though in the beginning, I'd encouraged her to confront her about sleeping with Sean, Drea didn't feel like that would be enough.

And then, one day, after catching Jerell cheating on me, again, I'd asked Drea to come over, and somehow, we shared something together that I'd never experienced. Neither of us had ever been with or into women.

Maybe we were both just lonely.

Maybe we were both just tired of men.

But she'd held me close to her chest that day, as I cried, and she'd told me that everything was going to be okay.

And then we ended up sharing something so passionate, so intimate, so intense…and it wasn't sex.

I'm not sure what it was.

Maybe it could be called foreplay. Or communicating threw touch. All I knew was that after that moment, my world became centered around her.

Were we just friends?

Or lovers?

We didn't know what we were. All we knew was that we meant the world to each other, and that's when things became complicated.

Somehow, Drea talked me into helping her get even with Lava.

At first, the plan was just to mess up their happy home. Start having an affair with West. Make him fall in love with me, again. And then, I would expose him. Lava would leave him, and their happy marriage would be destroyed.

The end.

That's it.

But the closer Lava and I became, the more and more she started to trust me, and then she started sharing secrets. At that point, it turned into something that it was never supposed to be.

The more that I told Drea, about her sister, the more she wanted to do. The more she wanted me to say. The more she wanted them to pay.

Having West fall in love with me, leave her, and then I leave him, just wasn't enough anymore.

And when we'd thought that she had killed Satin, or whoever she really was, Drea said that it was all too perfect. She'd said that Lava should spend the rest of her life in a jail cell, thinking about all of the things that she'd done.

So, she wanted me to use the secrets against her.

Honestly, no matter what Lava said or did, I'd always planned to turn in the recordings. I was just wasting time, waiting for the right moment. I'd had every intention of doing what made Drea happy.

I'd started to love her.

As strange as it was to me.

So, I did whatever she asked me to do.

But I hadn't expected Lava to fight back, and we hadn't expected Satin to be alive and not dead.

That was supposed to have worked, but her being alive messed up everything. And so, Drea told me to plant the ring, being that she was familiar with court and cases, she knew that that what I'd recorded about the fires, wouldn't be enough, to convince the police of what they'd done on its own, but somehow, Lava got out of that too.

Still, Drea was set on revenge.

Until...

One day, Kemp showed up, and the party was over.

Unless we wanted to end up dead.

I wasn't sure how he knew, but he'd shown up at the hotel, that day, waving a gun.

After starting all of this mess, Drea and I never met at each other's house. We always met at hotels to plot and plan.

It was obvious that Kemp had come to kill me.

Someone at the hotel had even given him a key to come inside of the room.

I remembered him pointing the gun at me, and then Drea came out of the bathroom.

Immediately, I could tell that he recognized her as Lava's sister.

Drea's presence saved my life.

Instead of shooting me, at gunpoint, he had a conversation with us instead.

He asked for details.

And out of fear, we told him everything.

In a weird sort of way, he seemed to understand Drea's pain. But that hadn't stopped him from telling us that it was time to move on and that we both had better stay the hell away from Lava.

And strangely, he'd told me that he had something for me. He also offered to do something for Drea too. To give her the peace that she'd been searching for, all of this time.

And he had.

Her husband was dead.

Her husband, Sean, had lived much longer than the doctors had expected him to. Actually, he'd been heading towards remission. It was a miracle that he was getting better. But Drea didn't think so.

She was disappointed.

She hadn't wanted him to live, but since it seemed as though he was, she'd filed for a divorce.

But that day, with Kemp offered to take care of her "problem", after she'd told him straight out that she'd wanted him dead, and that if he killed Sean, or had him killed, he would never have to worry about her bothering his precious Lava again.

He'd said okay.

Kemp had kept his word.

And we planned to keep ours.

I looked at her as she laid her chair back and covered her face with her arm.

She was leaving behind a lot more than I was.

Parents, sisters, a career, and friends.

On my end, I didn't have anyone.

I'd only had Jerell.

I hadn't seen him, since I'd had him to *mug* Lava, attack her and push her down, to make her lose the baby.

It had been him. He'd done it for me. And I'd arranged it because of Drea.

But Jerell hadn't done it for free.

I'd had to screw him for about two weeks, to thank him for the favor. And even though he knew that I wasn't going to take him back, he'd said that in the end, it was the least that he could do for me, after all that he had put me through.

The baby cooed, and I glanced back at him.

Oh yeah.

The baby.

That's what Kemp had for me.

He'd known so much about me that day.

He'd known that I couldn't get pregnant and have a baby of my own. He knew about my abortion and about all of the doctor visits with fertility specialists, so he offered to give me something that I'd always wanted.

He offered me a little family of my own.

A child.

It was the baby that Satin had gotten pregnant with, by George. He'd said that he'd planned to take the baby to him, but that he'd been sitting outside of George's house, watching him and his wife, gardening together.

He'd said that they looked so happy. They looked like they were in love. And that it wasn't his job to ruin someone else's story.

It was weird.

Kemp was like hot and cold.

The devil and an angel.

A lover…and a terrorist.

I'd never seen anything, or met anyone, quite like him before.

But he chose not expose George's affair, and so he offered to give the baby to me.

He gave me a son.

He had him brought to the hotel and once he placed him into my arms, he promised me that if me, or Drea ever went near Lava again, that he would kill both of us, and the baby.

And I knew that he would do it too.

So…

I turned the music up a little bit louder as I glanced at the signs, looking to go far, far away.

We were leaving, everything and everyone else behind.

I guess, on the bright side of things, everyone, in some way, had gotten what they'd wanted.

Especially Lava.

In the end, she had her husband back, and from the looks of it, they were going to be okay.

That was fine by me. Because the truth is:

I never really wanted her husband anyway.

****

The End

Check out these books next:

Her 13th Husband: https://amzn.to/2I5pCK3

The Hidden Wife: https://amzn.to/2FE5nO3

The Wrong Husband: https://amzn.to/2rfroyw

The Golden Lie: https://amzn.to/2FDiwXM

The Janes: https://amzn.to/2rhnCUl

Your Pastor My Husband: https://amzn.to/2rgDG96

THANKS FOR READING! CHECK OUT MORE OF MY BOOKS AND JOIN MY FACEBOOK GROUP AT:
https://www.facebook.com/groups/authorbmhardin/

For autographed paperbacks or writing services visit:

www.authorbmhardin.com

To contact: E-mail: bmhardinbooks@gmail.com